Leading the Way

Other Books in the Keystone Stables Series

A Horse to Love (Book One)
On the Victory Trail (Book Two)
Southern Belle's Special Gift (Book Three)
Summer Camp Adventure (Book Four)
Blue Ribbon Champ (Book Six)
Whispering Hope (Book Seven)
The Long Ride Home (Book Eight)

BOOK 5

KEYSTONE Stables

Formerly titled *The Winning Summer*

Marsha Hubler

ZONDERVAN.com/
AUTHORTRACKER
follow your favorite authors

Zonderkidz

Leading the Way
Formerly titled *The Winning Summer*

Requests for information should be addressed to:
Zonderkidz, *Grand Rapids, MI 49530*

Library of Congress Cataloging-in-Publication Data

Hubler, Marsha, 1947-
[Winning summer]
Leading the way / by Marsha Hubler.
p. cm. — (Keystone Stables ; bk. 5)
Summary: Although Skye has looked forward to teaching Katie, a blind camper, about riding and handling horses, Katie's bitterness over being blind and her parents' upcoming divorce challenge Skye's ability to teach and to share God's love.
ISBN 978-0-310-71796-6 (softcover)
[1. Blind—Fiction. 2. People with disabilities—Fiction. 3. Divorce—Fiction. 4. Horses—Fiction. 5. Christian life—Fiction. 6. Foster home care—Fiction.] I. Title.
PZ7.H86325Le 2010
[Fic]—dc22 2009010793

Interior illustrator: Lyn Boyer
Interior design and composition: Carlos Estrada and Sherri L. Hoffman

Printed in the United States of America

11 12 13 14 15 16 • 24 23 22 21 20 19 18 17 16 15 14 13 12 11 10 9 8 7 6 5 4 3

Dedicated to Christian Cochran, whose invaluable help made this book possible.

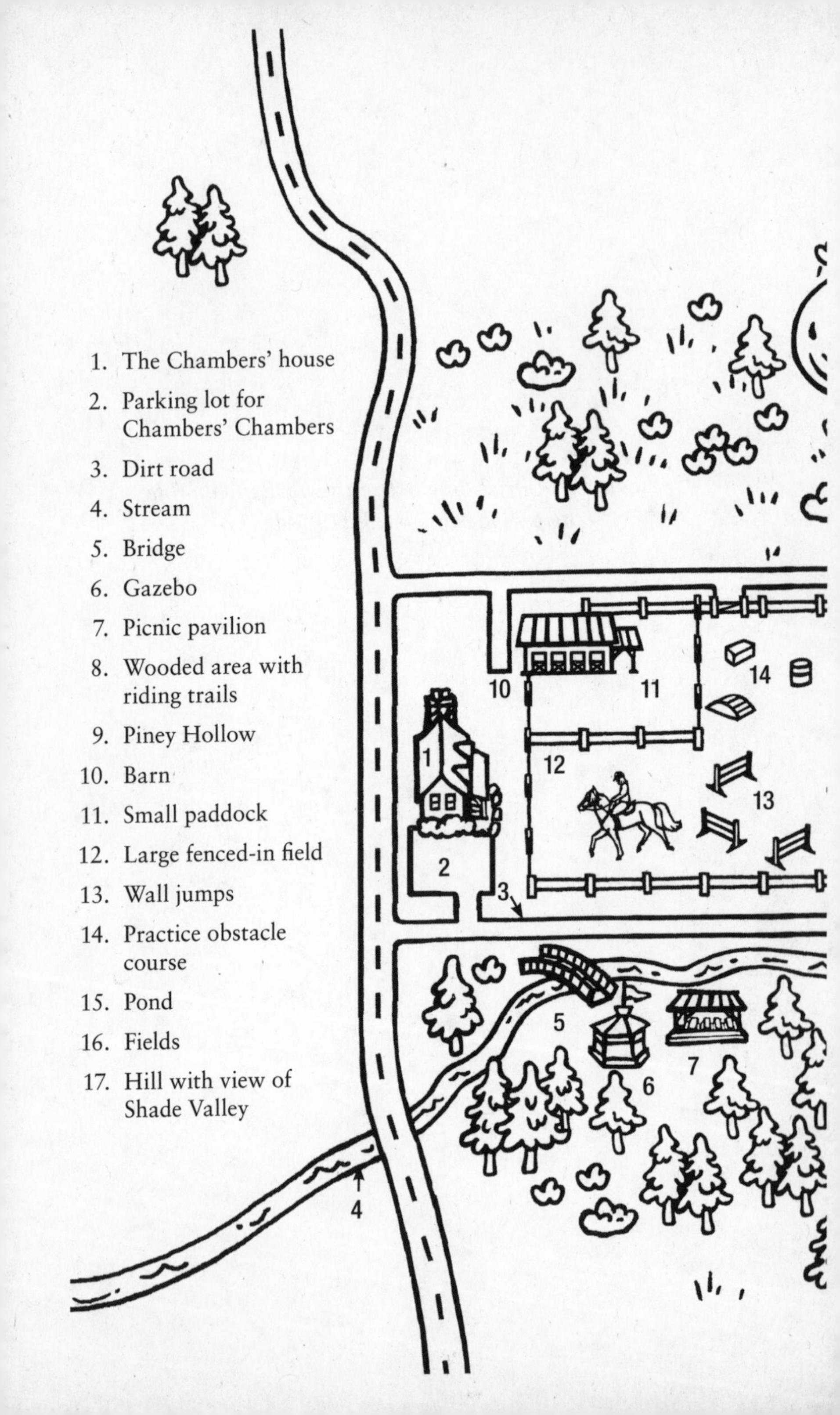
1. The Chambers' house
2. Parking lot for Chambers' Chambers
3. Dirt road
4. Stream
5. Bridge
6. Gazebo
7. Picnic pavilion
8. Wooded area with riding trails
9. Piney Hollow
10. Barn
11. Small paddock
12. Large fenced-in field
13. Wall jumps
14. Practice obstacle course
15. Pond
16. Fields
17. Hill with view of Shade Valley
1
2
3
4
5
6
7
10
11
12
13
14

Map of the Chambers' Ranch

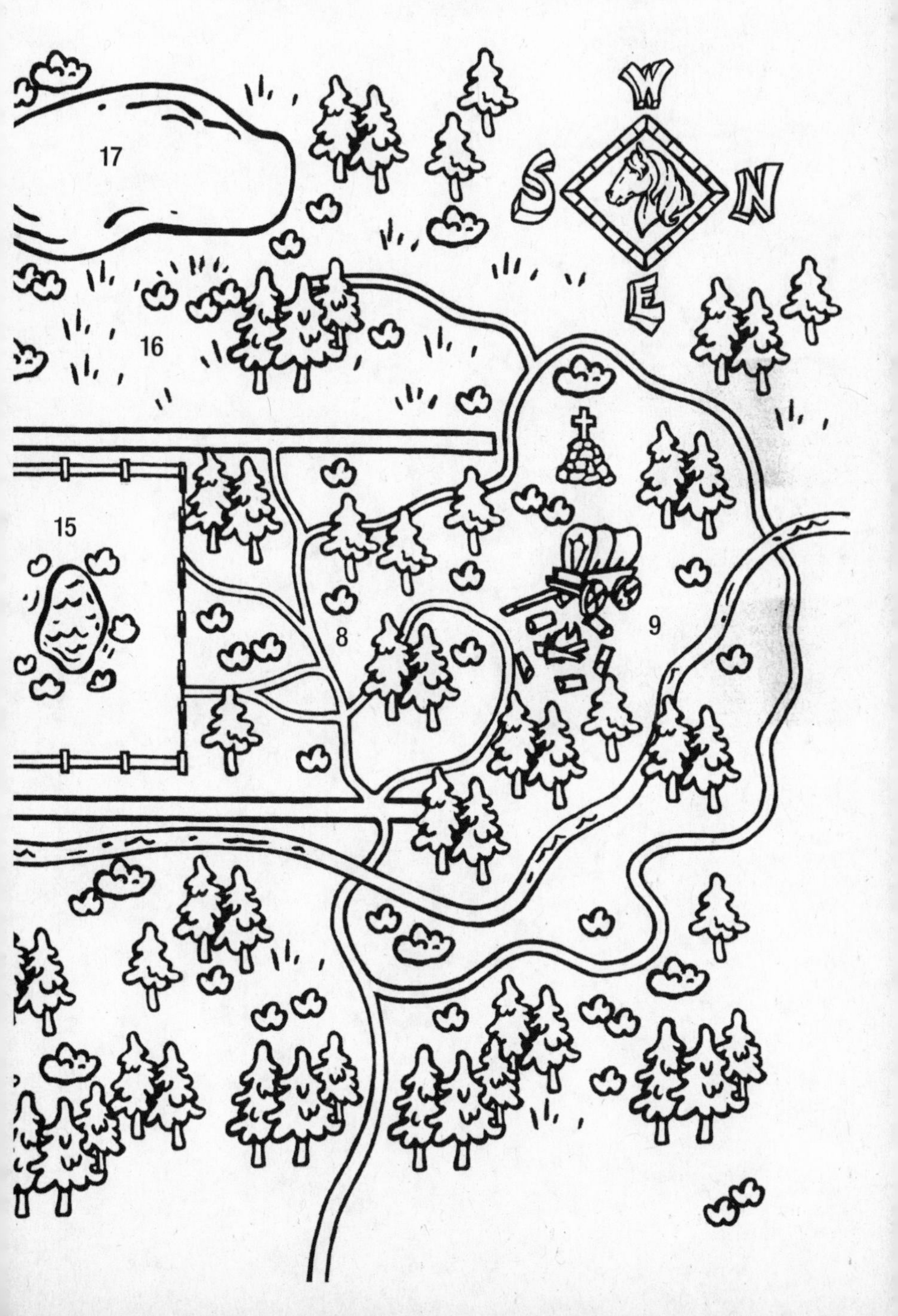

Skye, watch where you're going. You'll trip over the dogs!"

Along the railed walkway behind the house at Keystone Stables, Skye was feeling her way, eyes covered with a scarf.

"I can tell where they are," Skye said to Morgan, who followed in her wheelchair. "I can hear their nails clicking on the cement." Skye stopped, released her grip from the railing, and tentatively reached out to pet the dogs. "Here, Tippy! Here, Tyler!"

The Westies, delighted with even the least bit of attention, licked Skye's hands while their tails banged off her legs almost in unison. Behind Skye, the soft hum of Morgan's Jazzy came closer.

"How long are you going to do this?" Morgan asked impatiently. "You've been at it over a half hour, in the barn—and now in the backyard. Isn't that enough? I can think of much better ways to spend a hot Saturday afternoon. It's almost suppertime, Skye. We should be helping Mrs. C."

"Just a little while yet. If I'm going to be able to help Katie Thomas, I need to get a good idea of what it feels like to be totally blind." Skye reached behind her head and tightened the scarf's knot. "I want to go inside and see if I can find my way around my bedroom and the kitchen. I'll ask Mom if I can set the table."

"With your eyes covered?" Morgan laughed. "This should be a total riot. You'll probably drop every dish on the floor and smash your nose into the wall."

"Bet I won't! I know where everything is in the house. It'll be a piece of cake."

Again, Skye clung to the rail and started out, one cautious step at a time. Slowly, she made her way up the sloping sidewalk and ramp, onto the back porch of the house. She felt her way toward the sliding glass door.

"Should I open it for you?" Morgan asked.

"For Pete's sake, I'm not a cripple!" Skye shot off. "Oh, sorry."

"No problem." Morgan was already in deep thought. "I wonder if blind kids get frustrated like you just did. I mean, I'm sure they want to be as independent as possible, but I imagine people often treat them like they treat me. I sure don't like it."

"Well, we won't! Mom and Dad said every student has to pull his or her own weight. How many are coming tomorrow?"

"Four, bag and baggage, for three whole months. And Mr. C. is really excited about Katie. He says it's been a few years since Keystone Stables had a blind student who wanted to learn to ride."

Skye groped for the door handle. Sliding the door open, she stepped inside. Hands extended, she inched forward until she touched the back of a chair. "Okay, this is cool," she said, letting out a rush of nervous breath. "The dining room table is at twelve o'clock. Now the kitchen cupboards are to my— "

"Skye, what on earth are you doing?" Mrs. Chambers' voice rang out from the kitchen.

Skye turned her head to the left and smiled as though she could see Mrs. Chambers. "I'm pretending that I'm blind."

Newspaper pages fluttered at Skye's right. "That wouldn't have anything to do with Katie's coming tomorrow, would it?" Mr. Chambers said from the same direction.

Skye's head swiveled toward the man's voice. "Yep. I just thought this would help me understand how she feels."

Mrs. Chambers' words betrayed her thoughts. "What a unique way to try to understand someone."

Morgan motored in and closed the door. "I wouldn't mind if someone would try sitting in this chair all day long to understand me better. Of course, 'pretending' never quite cuts to all the problems special-needs kids have. At least Skye's trying to understand."

"I can certainly see that," Mrs. Chambers said with a chuckle, "and no pun intended. Well, if you want to do something in your present condition, Skye, I sure could use some help getting this meal ready."

"Could I set the table?" Skye asked.

"You may try!" Mrs. Chambers said.

"Be back in a few minutes." Morgan motored down the hallway and yelled a slight jab at Skye. "She said it would be a piece of cake!"

"But we're not having cake!" Mrs. Chambers yelled back and laughed.

"Smells like—" Mr. Chambers paused. "Hey, Skye, take a good whiff. What do you think we're having?"

"Hey, right!" Skye said. "I just read online that a blind kid's other four senses need to be really sharp to make up for not being able to see." She took a long deep breath, filling her nostrils with a blend of luscious aromas.

"What's the main course, Skye?" Mrs. Chambers asked.

Skye's mouth watered, and her stomach growled like a hungry bear. She inhaled deeply. "Smells like Tony's Pizzeria." She beamed. "Are we having pizza?"

"Pretty close," Mrs. Chambers said.

"Try again," Mr. Chambers said. "Maybe your ears can help."

Skye stood perfectly still, focusing her attention on the sounds coming from the kitchen. A faint bubbling from the stove competed with the soft hum of the refrigerator. "Something's boiling ... I know! It's got to be spaghetti noodles up to their necks in hot water. And I ... I smell sauce too. Right?"

"You get an A plus, honey," Mrs. Chambers said. "That's really quite good. Now, how about giving me a hand? The place mats are already laid out."

"Sure, Mom." Skye slid left around the table. She touched a chair and turned, reaching for a counter she knew was at arm's length from the chair. She edged her way along the counter to its end and stretched to her right, touching the refrigerator. She then reached up toward a cupboard where she knew the plates were kept.

"Just be careful," Mrs. Chambers added.

One step at a time, Skye began. For a task that usually took seconds, she struggled for fifteen minutes.

Her fingers felt their way inside cupboards and drawers. She retrieved what she thought were four large dinner plates, four napkins, and four complete sets of silverware. Edging her way back to the table, she maneuvered each object into what she thought was its rightful place. Finally, starting to make one more trip, she confidently balanced a tray of four empty glasses.

"How am I doing, Dad?" Skye said. "I told you this would be a piece of—"

Yipe! Yipe! Yipe!

Skye's foot smacked into a dog that, somehow, managed to be right in the girl's pathway. Skye heard yips and squeals, then nails clicking full speed ahead on the hardwood floor.

"Whoa!" Skye yelled as she stumbled forward, trying to balance the tray.

"Skye, look out!" Mr. Chambers yelled.

Skye's whole body flailed as she tried frantically to regain her footing. But it was too late. She felt herself heading somewhere—down and fast!

Suddenly, she felt a strong arm around her waist. The tray slipped out of her hands.

Crash! The awful sound of glass shattering on the floor echoed through the entire house.

Supported by the strong arm, Skye managed to regain her footing before crashing into something herself. She struggled and groped. At last, her hands found the back of a chair. She was shaking from head to toe.

"Honey, are you all right?" Mrs. Chambers' voice quivered as she wrapped her arm around Skye's shoulder. "I got her—just in time!" Mr. Chambers said as he released his strong grip around Skye's waist.

Still shaking, Skye gripped the back of the chair as though she'd never let go.

"I'm afraid you got a real taste of what it might be like to be blind," Mr. Chambers said. "If I hadn't caught you, you would have gone full force into the wall."

"What happened?" Morgan's voice echoed down the hall. "It sounded like an earthquake!"

"Skye dropped some glasses. But she's okay," Mrs. Chambers' relieved voice declared.

Lowering her head, Skye slowly untied the knot of her scarf. In deep thought, she stared at the mess on the table and the floor.

Totally blind! The reality of not being able to see—anything—whirled like a tornado in Skye's mind.

She felt so ashamed. "I am so sorry," she whispered.

"We're just glad you're not hurt," Mr. Chambers said, walking away. "I'll get the sweeper, and we'll clean up this mess."

"It must be terrible to be blind," Skye said. She brushed her long dark hair back from the sides of her face, seeing anew the beautiful scene beyond the sliding glass door. Down in the pasture, Skye's sorrel horse, Champ, nibbled at his evening meal in a field of brilliant green. "Blind kids have no idea what a horse even looks like."

Mrs. Chambers patted Skye's shoulder. "Not if they've been blind from birth. They have it pretty rough, Skye."

"But Katie lost her sight only four years ago in a car accident." Mr. Chambers carried in a dustpan, broom, and vacuum sweeper. "That might be worse—having known what everything looks like, and now not being able to see anything at all."

Morgan came down the hallway and stopped her Jazzy abruptly. "Wow! There's glass everywhere!"

Skye stared at her foster sister, noticing more freckles on Morgan's face than she ever thought she had.

"You know, I spend a lot of time thinking about different disabilities," Morgan said, flipping back her long, frizzy red hair. "I'd much rather have cerebral palsy than be blind."

"Why does God let it happen?" Skye asked. She looked into Mrs. Chambers' blue eyes, already moist with compassion.

"If we knew that answer, we'd be God," Mrs. Chambers said.

"Somehow, through all of their pain, people with disabilities are able to praise him anyway." Mr. Chambers ran fingers down both sides of his mustache then started to sweep glass shards into a dustpan. "God gives the strength."

"I sure don't know where I'd be without him," Morgan said with a smile, "or without Keystone Stables. Here's where I learned how to get my act together."

"Hopefully, if God blesses our work, we'll help other kids get their acts together," Mr. Chambers said. "Four more this summer."

"And teach them to praise the Lord through it all," Mrs. Chambers added.

"I'd sure like to help Katie in any way I can," Skye added, "but how do I do it?"

chapter two

Skye, this box has Katie's name on it." At the front door, Mr. Chambers handed Skye a backpack-sized cardboard box.

"I thought all her stuff was brought in when she and her mother set up the room earlier today," Skye said, struggling to balance it.

Mr. Chambers reached out a steadying hand. "You got it?"

"Yep," Skye said.

"Somehow, this one got all mixed up with the boys' boxes and suitcases," Mr. Chambers declared. "Please take it back to Katie's room while I help these guys get settled. Skye, this is Joey, Leonard, and Sam."

"Hi, guys," Skye said warmly.

"Hi," they said almost together.

Skye studied the three boys clustered together on the front porch and surrounded knee-deep in baggage. All younger than Skye, she guessed, each beamed a smile that overshadowed the trademark of his special needs: a helmet, leg braces, and thick glasses.

"I can't wait to see the horses," Joey bubbled.

"Me too," Leonard said. "I'm gonna ride all day every day!"

Mr. Chambers squared his cowboy hat and hoisted suitcases under each arm. He clutched two smaller bags in each hand. "Well, the sooner we get you guys settled, the sooner you'll get to see the horses."

Skye couldn't help giggling. "Dad, you look like a pack mule with a Stetson."

"Hmm ..." Mr. Chambers laughed. "A mule with a hat—and a mustache?"

The boys burst into hearty laughs. "That is too funny," Sam said. "A mule with a mustache."

"Do you have any horses with mustaches?" Leonard asked.

"Not with mustaches, but they do have beards," Mr. Chambers said.

"Beards?" Joey giggled.

"Well, kinda," Skye said. "They have whiskers, but we shave them off with an electric razor."

"What?" Sam said. "Ooh, I wanna see that."

"Me too," the other boys said.

"All in good time," Mr. Chambers said, stepping inside the house. "Just grab some suitcases and boxes. Let's get this show on the road!"

"And I'll take this box to its new home for the summer—special delivery!" Skye turned and hurried through the living room, down the hallway, and stopped at the doorway of Katie's room.

No Katie.

"Where is she?" Skye turned to her foster dad as he shuffled into the room across the hall.

"I think your mother took her down to the barn."

"Ooh, the barn!" Leonard yelled as he tagged after Mr. Chambers. "I can't wait."

"Just lay the box on Katie's bed," Mr. Chambers said. "I'm sure once she finds it, she'll know what it is, or what's in it."

"Okay, Dad." Skye entered the girl's room and placed the box on the bed next to a grocery bag full of snacks.

Turning to leave, her glance swept across the room and spotted a computer. Its screen saver flashed a kaleidoscope of colors.

"A computer?" Skye said. "A blind kid with a computer?"

Skye's curiosity, like a pin to a magnet, drew her to the computer station in the corner. Carefully, she reached down and jiggled the mouse. Relinquishing its colors, the screen revealed the beginning of a letter someone had been typing.

"Dear Dad ..." Skye read out loud. *But—how?*

She glanced at the keyboard, which looked the same as any other. "Okay, she knows how to type," Skye said, mumbling to herself, "but how does she know what's on the screen?"

Skye sat in front of the computer, examining the keyboard from left to right and back. Completely engrossed, she placed her fingers on the board.

H-e-l-l-o, she typed and then hit the space bar.

"Hello," an electronic voice said.

"You've got to be kidding!" Skye said. "This thing talks! Unbelievable!"

"What's unbelievable?" A girl's soft voice came from behind, launching Skye from the chair as though she had sat on a tack.

"Skye, what are you up to now?" Mrs. Chambers chided softly. "You know other kids' bedrooms are off-limits unless you're invited."

Skye turned toward the doorway. "I'm sorry. But this computer talks! That is so cool!"

"Skye, this is Katie Thomas. Katie, this is Skye Nicholson, one of our foster daughters."

The girls exchanged hellos. Skye studied the new girl.

Right hand holding a long thin cane, Katie leaned her plump body lazily against the door frame. Her blond hair, parted in the middle, framed a chubby face and hung freely, barely touching her shoulders. Bright green eyes, camouflaging her blindness, searched in the direction of the voice, appearing to study its owner as Skye studied back.

"Katie's mother wants her to learn how to ride this summer," Mrs. Chambers said. "That was Mrs. Thomas' last statement before she left."

"Even though I don't want to ride any dumb ol' horse," Katie said. "I'd rather just spend time with my stuff in my room."

"Well, we're glad you're here." Mrs. Chambers placed her hand on Katie's shoulder. "Now, I need to help Morgan finish getting supper ready. You two get to know each other a little better while the man of the house gets our boys settled in." Mrs. Chambers turned and left.

Katie touched the floor with the point of her cane. Sweeping it back and forth, she walked slowly into the room.

Skye rushed to her side and grabbed her arm. "Let me help you."

"For Pete's sake," Katie snapped. "I'm not a cripple!"

Skye pulled away abruptly. "Oh, I'm sorry. I—I— "

Katie stopped when her cane touched the bed. "Hey, look, I'm sorry I popped off. I know you meant well, but—well, thanks anyway."

"I can leave if you'd rather be alone," Skye said. *Morgan was right. People do treat blind people like they're crippled. I just did.*

"Nah, that's okay. My mother says I'm alone too much." Katie was already sitting on the bed. She reached into the grocery bag, pulled out a box, and grabbed a handful of crackers. She ate them like she hadn't eaten in a week. "Want some?"

"No, thanks," Skye said.

"Grab a seat somewhere if you'd like. Back home, there aren't any other blind kids in our school. I'm not exactly in the running for homecoming queen either. That's one reason Mom brought me here. She thinks it will be good for me to get to know a horse—personally. Sheesh!"

Skye straddled the chair as though she were climbing onto a horse. She folded her arms on the chair's back. "I just brought a box in. It's there on the bed next to your bag of goodies. What about your dad?"

"That's the other reason I'm here." Katie sighed and found the cardboard box. She opened it and felt the objects inside. "Hey, Mom thought we left this box at home. I'll have to call and let her know that all my electronic stuff is here. Great!" She started pulling out the items and laying them on the bed.

"Katie, what about your dad?"

"Oh, yeah. You might as well know that my parents aren't living together, and they're gonna get a divorce. It's my fault. I know it is."

"Why do you say that?"

"Let's just say that I haven't been the perfect daughter since my accident four years ago. I hate being blind, and I let everyone know it. My straight A's went down the tubes along with all my sports, cheerleading, and other activities. Oh, yes, and let's not forget my very good friends who never come around at all anymore." Katie rummaged roughly through the box and slammed the flaps shut. She grabbed another handful of crackers and gobbled them down.

"Don't you go to church?" Skye asked, staring at all the equipment on the bed.

"When I have to." Katie's tone darkened. "There aren't any blind kids there either."

"Aren't you a Christian?"

"Yeah, I am. But God and I aren't exactly on good terms since my accident. He could have prevented it, you know. I kinda put him in the same category with all my other friends who deserted me."

"Wow," Skye said with alarm. "Not having God on your side sounds pretty scary to me. I don't know what I'd do if I couldn't go to him with all my problems."

"Well, you're not blind," Katie said sarcastically but then quickly changed her tone. "Anyway, do you wanna see some of my stuff?"

"Yeah, if you wanna show it to me."

Katie stood and reached toward the computer.

Skye stood. "You can sit here if you want."

"No, no. You stay there. I'll give you a demonstration. You can be my audience." Katie's face beamed with pride as she fingered the printer next to the computer. "Now, this computer system has special programs. Wait until you see what it can do. There should be a pile of books to your right, Skye. Grab one and open it to any page."

Skye handed Katie an open book.

Katie punched a few keys on the keyboard and a program called Kurzweil appeared on the screen. She placed the open book in its appropriate place on the printer/scanner and poked a button. In seconds, the machine scanned the entire page into the computer, and a distinguishable electronic voice started reading the first sentence.

"How about that?" Katie's round red cheeks sported half a smile. "I call this electronic voice Cindy. She's what you call a speech engine. We spend a lot of time together, so I figure she needs a name. I can put any book, any page, in the scanner. If a book doesn't come in Braille or as a CD or cassette, this is how I do my homework."

Skye stared, her mouth open in disbelief. "I had no idea blind kids had things like this to help them."

"Wait until I show you the stuff on the bed." Katie bubbled with enthusiasm. "I have a calculator, a clock, and a dictionary, and they all talk. I even have a Braille Scrabble game. Do you like to play Scrabble?"

"Yeah, I love it," Skye answered.

Katie reached over to the bed and retrieved a device about the size of a Walkman. "This is my very favoritist one of all."

"What is it?"

"It's called a book port." Katie fingered it fondly. "With this little baby I can download e-books from the Internet using a standard USB port, and I can record music files from CDs. I can also put textbooks on here if they're available as e-texts or digital talking books. This thing has eight different voices. I like Ricochet Randy the best. Oh, this is the best part. If there's a book loaded in here, I can find any chapter, line, or word in the book with a key command. All I do is plug it into my speaker or headset, and I'm ready for hours of entertainment."

"That's unreal," Skye said. "So you don't really need the books in Braille?"

"Lots of times the books aren't in Braille. That's when I really need this book port." Katie beamed the broadest of smiles. "When I tell people my favorite hobby is reading, I can imagine the kinds of faces they're making. But I love to 'read.'"

"Then with all this neat stuff, how come you're not getting A's in school anymore?"

"Well—I—" Katie said.

"Girls, supper's ready!" Mrs. Chambers' voice carried all the way from the kitchen.

"I'll tell you later," she said. "Let's go. I'm starved!"

"Hey, thanks for showing me all your stuff anyway." Skye stood. "After we eat, I want to show you my favorite hobby. It isn't an it; it's a he, and he has a room down in the barn."

"Let me guess." Katie grinned mischievously as she stood. "Could 'it' possibly be a pig?"

The girls laughed as they walked together out of the room.

chapter three

Hey, Mom," Skye said as she and Katie entered the dining room. "I thought you said supper was ready. There's nothing on the table but a vase of wildflowers. I'm not hungry for weeds and seeds!"

Skye and Katie giggled as they stopped at the table.

"I have a little surprise for you two." Mrs. Chambers glanced at the girls while she packed sandwiches into a basket.

Morgan busied herself taking cans of soda from the refrigerator and putting them in a small cooler. "Katie, do you like picnics?"

"Do I?" Katie said. "Picnics are absolutely my favoritist way to eat. Where are we going?"

"I have a feeling it won't be far," Skye said. "It's probably within walking distance. Right, Mom?"

"You guessed it. We're walking over to our own picnic grove," Mrs. Chambers said. "What desserts would you girls like? Brownies, chocolate chip cookies, or pecan pie?"

"You know I'm a brownie addict," Skye said.

"Chocolate chip cookies for me," Morgan said.

"I'll sample all of them." Katie's round face beamed. "In the house or out, desserts are the best part of any meal."

And you look like you could eat them all, Skye thought.

"C'mon, desserts, you're invited." Mrs. Chambers laughed as she stuffed the basket and then glanced at the girls again. "I don't want the pecan pie to get a complex in here all by itself. Skye, why don't you two head over to the picnic grove? Morgan and I will be along shortly."

"Where are the boys—and Dad?" Skye asked.

Morgan motored to the table, placed the cooler on it, and reached to the counter for a bag of chips. "You know he's a picnicking nut too. He took the boys in the truck back to Piney Hollow. They're gonna do their macho thing."

"In fact," Mrs. Chambers added, "tonight they're sleeping in a pup tent back there. Tom said he couldn't see such a crystal-clear day, or night, going to waste. He loves camping out under the stars, so the four of them will be roughin' it."

"Where—what—is Piney Hollow?" Katie asked.

"It is so cool," Skye said. "It's a campsite in the back of this place. It has a chuck wagon and outdoor chapel and everything. We have youth retreats there sometimes."

"And meals cooked on an open fire." Morgan flipped her hair back. "Your little ol' taste buds never had it so good."

"Ummm, I'm for that," Katie said. "When do we get to do that?"

Mrs. Chambers finished packing the picnic-ware. "We weren't quite sure you'd enjoy that, Katie. Your mother says that you spend most of the time with your equipment in the bedroom. But—"

"Well, I'd sure like to try camping." Katie's whole face lit up. "That sounds so cool. And I'd love to try the food. I've never had anything cooked on an open fire."

"Then you haven't lived." Skye could hardly contain herself. "Wait until you taste bacon and eggs and—"

"Skye, let's take care of one meal at a time," Mrs. Chambers said. "Right now we're going to have cold sandwiches—without a fire! Now you two get going."

"Okay, Mom," Skye said, tugging at Katie's shirt-sleeve. "C'mon, Katie."

"Just let me grab your elbow, and I'll follow, okay?" Katie folded her cane into four smaller sections and stuffed it into a nylon pouch that hung from her belt.

"Hey, that cane is neat. I didn't know you could fold it like that," Skye said. "What's it made of?"

"Graphite," Katie answered. "Light as a feather but strong enough to take a lot of grief from a kid like me."

In another frenzy of giggles, the two girls made their way out the sliding door and down the porch ramp. To their right, they followed the sidewalk that bordered the white pasture fence, Skye acquainting Katie with the grounds every step of the way.

"Hey, let's stop here for a minute," Skye said. "I told you I wanted you to meet someone. We don't have to wait until after supper."

"You mean it's time to meet your pig?" Katie laughed.

"Yeah." Skye played along with Katie. "I want you to meet Oinkers."

Skye stuck two fingers in her mouth and let out a shrill whistle.

From the bottom of the pasture, a small herd of horses started galloping. Up through the field they came, long manes and tails bouncing with the thrill of the run. The ground rumbled with the beat of six sets of hooves. At the front of the herd ran a smaller horse, as fast as the wind and shining like a brand-new penny.

Clinging tightly to Skye's arm, Katie moved back. "That sounds like more than one horse, Skye. And they sound dangerous. Are they gonna run over me?"

"No, you're fine." Skye slipped her arm away from Katie and took a step forward. "There's a big white fence between them and us."

In seconds, the horses lined up along the fence, their heads bobbing over the top rail and reaching toward the girls.

Skye reached out and grabbed Champ's halter. "Katie, I'll introduce you to the horses, one at a time."

Katie took another step back. "I really don't need to meet any stinkin' horses. Let's go."

"Aw, c'mon. There are only six of them." Skye was beaming with pride. "They won't hurt you. Here, grab my arm, and I'll move you a little closer."

"Um, I don't know— "

"Like it or not, you came here to learn to ride. Well, guess what? You have to touch a horse before you climb on one. Here, reach out, and I'll let you pet my horse, Champ. He's reddish brown and the best horse that ever lived."

Katie edged her hand forward as if feeling the heat from a red-hot stove. "I—I don't like this," she said. "I've never been around horses. You don't exactly see them in the city every day."

"He won't hurt you," Skye promised. "Just feel how soft he is."

Katie reached a little farther, her hand finally coming to rest on Champ's velvety soft nose. He nickered, and Katie pulled back. "What was that?"

"That's Champ's way of saying hello," Skye said. "Isn't he soft?"

"Well, yeah." This time Katie reached with less reluctance. "And fuzzy. He kinda feels like my stuffed animals."

"Now do you wanna meet the others?"

Without waiting, Skye grabbed each horse by the halter one at a time, letting Katie touch each one. Finally, they came to the last horse.

"Now, this little guy's name is Boomerang," Skye said. "His breed is Pinto. I think Mom and Dad want you to learn to ride him. He's as gentle as a lamb, and he's very good with beginners. We call him 'Boomer' for short."

With growing confidence, Katie reached out to pet him. "Why do you call him Boomerang? And what's a Pinto horse?"

"Well, he's our barrel-racing horse. And he's so fast, he reminds us of a boomerang going down and back. A Pinto is either brown and white or black and white. Boomer is brown and white."

"What's barrel racing?" Katie's curiosity had finally gotten the best of her.

"It's an event in horse shows and rodeos. Three barrels are set up in a cloverleaf pattern in a corral. When the horse and rider charge into the arena, a clock times how fast the team can run around the barrels and cross a finish line. This fella and Mom have won blue ribbons in that event. Even though he's a small Quarter Horse, he is one fast dude. He's almost as fast as Champ."

"And they're gonna stick me on a horse like that? No way."

"He won't barrel race with you," Skye said. "When you're taking lessons, he'll just walk around slowly in the corral. Just wait, you'll see. Boomer's a perfect gentleman with the ladies."

"Does Champ barrel race?"

"No, he does other events."

"Did he ever win anything?"

"Sure. He has lots of blue ribbons too."

"Wow. That is so neat." Katie edged her body forward. "Can I get closer to Boomerang?"

"Yep," Skye said. "Here, let me help you."

Slowly, Katie moved her hands forward. Skye held Boomer's halter while the blind girl's fingers wiggled freely, coming to rest on the horse's receptive nose. She felt the horse as though sculpting a piece of clay. Her hands crept upward, gently feeling the strength of his face and forehead and the stiffness of his long eyelashes that closed over large Bambi eyes. Her hands slid down both sides of his face, over his strong cheekbones and halter, and down around his velvet muzzle and fuzzy chin.

"His lips are furry! Wow! I never imagined a horse would feel like this," Katie said. "All I ever knew was that they were big. But he's—he's gorgeous!"

"His color and markings are gorgeous too," Skye said. "His head's brown except for a white blaze. That's a stripe down the middle of his face. His mane and tail are white with black mixed in. The rest of him is massive blotches of brown on white. He is one pretty picture."

"Oh, I wish I could see him," Katie said.

"Well, you can—in your own way," Skye said. "Feeling Boomer is a lot more than most city kids have the chance to do."

Skye looked toward the picnic grove and suddenly remembered where they were headed in the first place. "We'd better get going. Mom and Morgan will probably be out in a sec." She turned toward the horses. "You guys can go finish your supper now!"

As the girls made their way along the fence, the horses turned back into the pasture, each one finding its own spot of grass to nibble. Skye and Katie came to the end of the walk, crossed a dirt road, walked over a bridge that straddled a small stream, and stopped at the pavilion nestled in a cluster of tall pine trees.

Skye led Katie to the picnic table. As Katie sat, Skye stood at the end of the table and studied the scene before her. Her brown eyes darted in a dozen different directions, capturing the beauty of the perfect June day. She took a deep breath of pine scent and then glanced back at the horses enjoying their evening meal. Her glance drifted closer to where she stood, to a gazebo resting near the pavilion, and she studied the intricate designs cut into the fancy wood. She looked up, feasting on the brilliant blue sky, absorbing the entire scene.

"Will you look at that cool sky?" Skye caught herself the second the words slipped from her mouth. "Oh, Katie, I'm sorry."

"No problem," Katie said, letting out a long sigh. "I get that all the time. People will say, 'Oh, look at that' or 'Can't you see that,' but of course, I can't. I'm almost used to it. And I do remember what blue looks like. The best skies are the ones with big, puffy white clouds. One of my favoritist things to do was lie in the yard at home and look for dragons and— "

A long pause preceded Skye's attempt to speak. "Katie ..."

With a frown on her face, Katie sat still, her pudgy body humped over like an old woman.

"Hey, is there any chance you might ever get your sight back?" Skye's excitement was obvious in her voice. "I mean, they do all kinds of neat operations to help people see."

"My mom's had me all over the place to find out. We've seen zillions of specialists. They all say there's really nothing wrong with my eyes."

Skye frowned, deep in thought. "There's nothing wrong with your eyes? Then what's making you blind?"

"The damage was done to my brain. One doctor said that if he could perfect a certain kind of surgery on that part of the brain, there might be a slim chance that I could see again. I live for that day. But Mom keeps telling me not to get my hopes up. Well, she's not blind!"

"God could perform a miracle," Skye said.

"Miracle? What miracle?" Mrs. Chambers asked from behind.

Morgan followed, carrying the picnic supplies on her lap.

"To give Katie her sight back," Skye said. "Jesus did it when he was here on earth. Why couldn't he do it for Katie?"

Straightening her back, Katie turned toward the voices.

"Well," Mrs. Chambers said, placing the basket on the table, "that's something we can all pray about. In the meantime, let's enjoy God's creation and the food he's given us. And while we're on that subject, right now we should pray for our meal."

Morgan maneuvered her wheelchair to the end of the table and laughed. "Mrs. C., are you sure we should pray about this meal, especially since we're going to indulge in all those luscious desserts? We'll probably each gain five pounds just looking at them. That sounds sort of sinful to me."

Everyone laughed.

"Who cares if we gain five or ten pounds? I sure don't!" Katie declared. "Bring 'em on!"

It was Monday morning at Keystone Stables and time for riding lessons! By nine o'clock the hot June sun had already posted its warning for another scorcher of a day.

Skye and Katie rested their arms over the top rail of the small riding corral. Katie was devouring a candy bar. Next to the barn, Mr. Chambers and Morgan were showing Joey and Leonard, wearing helmets, how to saddle and bridle their horses. In the corral, a young man, looking sharp in western attire including a black Stetson, led a brown horse. Sam, also wearing a helmet, sat in the saddle and held on for dear life. As the young man walked the team in a circle, Skye's heart went with him.

Chad, you are so sweet. Skye's whole being smiled.

"What's goin' on now?" Katie asked, finishing her candy. "If everyone's too busy, I can just wait. I don't need to do this today."

"Like Mom and Dad said earlier, Katie, today *you* should take your first ride," Skye insisted. "So I guess you do need to do this today. And it will be your turn as soon as Chad's done giving Sam his first lesson."

"This is so dumb," Katie snapped, then changed her tone. "Who's Chad?"

"The sweetest boy this side of heaven," Skye whispered. "He's fifteen and in our youth group and blond and super cute!"

"He's your boyfriend?"

"Nah. Mom and Dad say I'm way too young to be thinking of boyfriends. And Chad's too busy for girls. He has a part-time job and he plays the guitar and practices preaching to the youth group at church and— "

"Wow, you really like him, don't you?" Katie asked. "Is there anything about him you don't know?"

Chad led the horse team past the two girls. "Hey, Skye, looks like we'll see a lot of each other this summer, thanks to Mr. C. I can always use the extra money for my college fund!"

Gulp! Skye felt her face turn red-hot as her mind went blank. Staring at Chad was the only thing she could do.

"Skye," Katie said, reaching to her side, "are you there?" Her hand found Skye's arm. "Answer the man! You sure had enough to say about him just a second ago!"

Chad burst into a hearty laugh as he led the horse team to the other side of the corral. "Skye, you've only been in the sun a few minutes, and you already have quite a burn. Better get some sunscreen!"

"C'mon, Katie!" Skye grabbed her arm. "It's time for your lesson—now!"

"I don't want to!" Katie sounded off.

"Well, want to or not, now's the time. C'mon." Skye led Katie inside the barn where Mrs. Chambers had just finished cross-tying Boomer in the open hall. Seeing the two girls, she slipped into a nearby stall and came out carrying a hard hat and a bucket filled with grooming gear.

Skye took the helmet from Mrs. Chambers. "Okay, Katie, time for your first lesson. Here's your hard hat."

Skye gently set the helmet on Katie's head.

"What's that for?" Katie felt the helmet.

"State regulations," Mrs. Chambers explained in no-nonsense terms. She walked next to Boomer and placed the bucket down. "There are all kinds of ways you could hurt your head. This rule is a good one."

"I bet I really look dumb," Katie lamented.

"All the students have to wear them," Skye said. "It won't take long to get used to. There's a chin strap for you to snap shut."

"Oh, then it must look a lot like a bike helmet." Katie snapped the chin strap in place.

"Kinda," Skye said.

"For once I'm glad I can't see," Katie joked. "I looked weird in my helmet when I rode my bike. Do the horses have to wear them too?"

Skye forced out a laugh. "Very funny. Although it probably wouldn't hurt, the way some of the students act."

Mrs. Chambers pulled a currycomb from the bucket. "That's right. It never pays to be rough with horses. The gentler you are with them, the gentler they'll be with you. Okay, Katie, here's what we're going to do. Let Skye bring you right next to Boomer. I'll give you a currycomb, and we'll show you how to brush a horse."

A shroud of worry covered Katie's face. "Is there a fence between us like yesterday?"

"No, but it's okay. He's really gentle."

"I—I don't think I want to do this." Katie took a step back.

"We'll be right here with you," Mrs. Chambers said. "Boomer's tied, so he can't walk away or step on you. I'll hold him real steady while Skye shows you what to do. C'mon, try it. I think you'll like it."

"This is still dumb, but all right." Katie's voice relaxed a little

Skye turned to her. "Do you want my arm?"

"No, I'll try it myself," Katie said.

Side by side the girls edged forward. Mrs. Chambers handed Skye the comb and held the horse's head steady.

"Reach forward and feel how tall he is. He's just right for you," Skye said.

Slowly Katie reached her hand forward. "Wow! He is so smooth! Just like a silk blouse my mother has. Hey, he really isn't that big after all." She leaned cautiously against Boomer's withers. "Look, I can rest my head on his back. And he smells good too!"

"The best smell in the whole universe, as far as I'm concerned," Skye said, patting Boomer's neck. "He feels smooth because in the summer, most horses have really short hair. They only look like fuzzy bears in the winter. Reach to your left to his neck. Then run your hands along his back, belly, and rump. See how firm he is from all the running he does? This guy's all muscle."

"Well, I sure hope he doesn't do any running with me." Carefully, Katie slid her hands all over the horse. "Where's the saddle? I won't get on him without a saddle!"

"That will come in good time," Mrs. Chambers said. "First we want you to feel comfortable around Boomer. You need to get to know each other."

Skye gave Katie the comb and guided her hand up to Boomer's head. "Here. Now I'll teach you how to curry him. He absolutely loves it. Start up here at his neck, in back of the halter, and brush in downward strokes. Then work your way onto his back, belly, rump, and his legs."

"Then you can do the same on his other side," Mrs. Chambers said. "But never walk behind a horse. Always go to the other side by going around his head."

"Why?" Katie asked.

Mrs. Chambers continued, "Although Boomer never would, some horses kick for no reason at all. A horse's kick is powerful enough to send you through a wall."

"Wow," Katie said. "Are they that strong?"

"Yeah, and that's not something you want to find out the hard way." Skye pulled a large brush from the bucket and placed it in Katie's hand. "Here's a brush to use on him too. That really makes his coat shine."

Mrs. Chambers tightened her grip on the horse's halter as Katie felt her way to begin. "This is the best way to bond with a horse," Mrs. Chambers said. "If Boomer knows that you like him, he'll do anything you ask when you're on his back. You're not afraid of him now, are you?"

"No, not really." Katie combed the horse in deliberate, long strokes. Her giggle sounded shaky. "I'm just a little nervous, that's all."

"Horses can sense when you're nervous," Skye said. "Just try to relax and have a good time. Remember, Boomer's a perfect gentleman around ladies."

Mrs. Chambers released the horse's halter and moved away. "I think they'll be fine, Skye. I want to see how Tom and Chad are doing with the boys. You two go ahead and love this little guy. Butter him up! I'll be back in a minute."

Standing next to Katie, Skye tried to put her at ease. "Now we'll find out if you're a kid who can pat your head and rub your tummy at the same time. Try brushing with one hand and combing with the other. I'll be right here beside you. In a few weeks, after you get to know him better, we'll show you how to clean his front hooves."

"Clean his hooves?" Katie asked. "Why would I want to do that—and how?"

"Well," Skye said, "all four hooves need to be cleaned on the bottom every day. If dirt and manure stay wedged in parts of the hoof called the frog, the horse can get an infection called thrush and go lame. I wouldn't want you to mess with his back feet, but it's easy to do his front ones. Boomer's so well trained, all you have to do is touch his knee, and he lifts his hoof. I'm sure you can learn to clean his hooves, and I'll be here to help you every step of the way."

"Wow. What do you use to clean them? And how do you do it?"

"A metal pick. You have to bend the leg up and pry out all that caked dirt."

Deep in thought, Katie stopped grooming and laid both arms across Boomer's back. "I had no idea horses needed all this TLC."

"Well, they do," Skye said, "and they need lots of space too, not only to keep them, but to ride them."

"Speaking of riding, where—and when—will I have to ride him?"

"Out in the small paddock where Chad and Sam are now. I think Mom wants you to try it today. What do you think?"

As if the horse understood what Skye had said, he turned his head toward Katie, nodded, and let out a hearty neigh.

Startled, Katie jumped back. Skye reached out to steady the girl.

"Wow! That was loud!" Katie said in a nervous voice. "I—I don't think I'm ready for this, Skye."

"Katie, get with it!" Skye ordered. "Get ready to ride, or get ready to be grounded."

In about a half hour, Skye and Katie had finished grooming Boomer. Skye had tacked the horse—and had convinced Katie it was in her best interest to get on the horse. As the girls walked Boomer out of the barn, they passed Chad and his team on their way in.

"You did a great job for your first lesson," Chad said to Sam, still in the saddle.

"I like it," Sam replied. "Can I do it some more?"

"I'm afraid not," Chad said. "We have to give the corral to the girls for a while." Beautiful brown eyes peeking from under his Stetson, Chad winked and his dimples radiated a cordial smile. "It's all yours, ladies!"

"Thanks, Chad." Skye smiled back as she led Boomer on her right and Katie on her left. "Hey, Chad, I almost forgot. Mom said she has lemonade and cookies in the kitchen."

"Now you're talking." Chad's voice trailed away into the barn's interior.

"Leave some for me! That is, if I come out of this alive!" Katie yelled back.

Skye walked her team from the coolness of the barn into the growing heat of the humid day. In the corral, they met Mrs. Chambers.

"We think you're ready to try this, Katie. What do you think?" Mrs. Chambers spoke confidently. "We'll take it real slow. Skye will be leading Boomer every step of the way."

"All we're gonna do is walk around the perimeter of the corral until you get the feel of the saddle," Skye said. "Give me your hand, Katie."

Skye placed a sugar cube in the girl's open hand.

"What's that?" Katie asked.

Mrs. Chambers checked the bit in Boomer's mouth. "It's a sugar cube, Katie. Horses will practically sit up and beg to get sugar cubes. That's their candy!"

Skye turned Katie toward the left side of the horse. "Now, just stand here a sec and watch what happens. Horses can smell sugar a mile away."

Katie stood perfectly still.

"Hold the sugar toward Boomer's head," Skye said. "Open your hand wide with the sugar in your flat palm."

Katie held her hand out.

Boomer turned his head back and gently nibbled the cube from Katie's hand, leaving a deposit of wet foam on her hand. His teeth made loud crunching sounds. Katie giggled.

"He took it!" Katie wiped her hand on her jeans. "He took it—and that tickled."

Skye and Mrs. Chambers gave each other a smile.

"Sure he took it," Skye said. "Now he knows who his real friend is—you. We'll give you a few cubes every time you ride, and you'll have him dancing in circles."

"He doesn't really dance, does he?" Katie's tone was skeptical.

Mrs. Chambers checked the cinch on the saddle. "Not yet," she joked. "But he's quite a horse. Maybe— "

"Mom!" Skye interrupted. "Katie, just so you know, none of our horses really dance."

"Do any horses dance?" Katie's curiosity was real.

"Well," Skye said, "I guess you could say Lipizzaners and Andalusians 'dance.' They do all kinds of fancy footwork when they perform. But that takes years of special training."

"Hey," Katie said, "maybe we could look it up on the Internet. I'd like to know more about them."

"Right now you'll have enough to do to learn more about this horse," Mrs. Chambers said.

Not to be ignored, Boomer turned back to Katie, this time licking her arms, nudging her with his exploring nose. Katie automatically took a step back, but then she paused. Stepping forward, she carefully reached toward the horse. He sniffed her, and as he started licking, Katie's arms found their way around his neck, and she gave the friendly horse a warm embrace.

"Boomer," she declared, "whether you can dance or not, maybe we can be friends after all!"

chapter five

"Please pass the rolls." Skye examined the table loaded with fried chicken, baked potatoes, corn, and applesauce—all her favorite foods.

Mrs. Chambers handed the rolls to Skye and glanced at Katie's mother. "Mrs. Thomas, we're so glad you could visit today."

"Please call me Christine." The woman forced a smile after she took a quick sip of coffee. She fingered shoulder-length frizzed hair that framed a thin face engraved with worry. "This is the first Sunday I've had off in weeks. I'm just glad I was able to get away."

Buttering her roll, Skye watched Katie, who appeared engrossed in her plate piled high with food. The expression on her face registered a blank.

"You work at an envelope factory, isn't that right?" Mrs. Chambers knew how to get the conversation going.

"Yes," Mrs. Thomas said. "In the office. I do the payroll. It can be a demanding job. It never bothered me until the guys in the front office decided to work the factory on Sundays. I hate missing church. And if I don't get there, Katie usually doesn't either."

Katie managed a look of disdain, even with her cheeks working on a mouthful of food. She never said a word.

What's with her? Skye pondered. *She sure is different when her mom's around.*

Mrs. Thomas quickly changed the subject. "Where's your other girl? And your husband?"

"Morgan is visiting a friend," Mrs. Chambers said. "She'll be back sometime before supper. Tom took our other students on a nature hike and hot-dog roast. He loves the outdoors. They'll be back tonight, ready to face a busy week."

Skye sipped her lemonade. "Morgan and I will definitely need our beauty sleep tonight. We have orders to clean our bedrooms tomorrow. That'll take most of the day. Of course, we can't start tearing the rooms apart until we've finished giving riding lessons in the morning."

"And how's Katie doing with her lessons?" Mrs. Thomas took a bite of a roll.

"Just fine!" Katie snapped. "When's Dad comin' to see me?"

Skye's eyebrows peaked as she glanced in Mrs. Chambers' direction.

Mrs. Chambers, as usual, chose her words with care. "Katie's doing a marvelous job. For only two weeks of lessons, you'd think she was born on a horse. She's a natural!"

"Boomer's a great horse," Katie snapped again. "He makes it easy to learn. Mom, you didn't answer me. When's Dad coming?"

Mrs. Thomas sighed. "Katie, I just don't know. He won't return my calls. The last time I talked to him, he said he'd try to visit at the end of the month. So maybe next weekend— "

"I wanna show him how I can ride," Katie interrupted. "Why didn't you come together?"

Mrs. Thomas placed her fork down and folded her arms. "Katie, you know that's impossible." She looked at

Mrs. Chambers. "This last year hasn't been easy—for any of us. The last time the three of us were together, all we did was argue over money and whose fault Katie's accident was. We blamed each other and kept going in circles. If it weren't for our 'Others Fund' at church, Katie wouldn't be here for the summer. It never would have fit into our budget."

"More chicken, anyone?" Mrs. Chambers smiled as she passed the plate. "Christine, have you sought any professional help?"

"They won't!" Katie piped in. "She won't! They don't think it's worth it." Her voice then became subdued. "I'll take more chicken."

"The plate's to your immediate left," Mrs. Chambers said, handing Katie the chicken.

Katie took two more pieces and started right in on them.

"This is something Katie doesn't understand." Mrs. Thomas directed her words to Mrs. Chambers. "We've gone to our pastor—on several occasions. But it hasn't helped. Keith is a mechanic, and our incomes are, well, let's just say, we don't have money for seventy-dollar-an-hour counselors. Keith figured it was just easier to leave."

"And you didn't try to stop him either!" Katie complained.

Mrs. Thomas let out another long sigh. "Sometimes you just get tired of fighting it."

"You guys don't care about me, or you would try!" Katie shoved a forkful of food into her mouth.

Wow! If I talked like that to Mom, I'd be grounded forever! Skye focused on eating her chicken leg.

Determined to change the mood, Mrs. Chambers smiled all the way to her blue eyes. "Katie, your mother seems very interested in your riding progress. What do you say we get Boomer out this afternoon so you can give a demonstration?"

"Okay." Katie nodded.

For the first time since sitting down, Mrs. Thomas seemed to relax. She shot a glance in her daughter's direction. "I'd love to see you ride that horse, Katie. I'd like you to show me everything you've learned."

No answer from Katie.

Skye wiped her mouth with a napkin and jumped in to help things along. "You could show her how to groom him and clean his hooves and everything!"

Mrs. Chambers sipped her coffee. "The biggest surprise you'll find is that Katie can ride Boomer without anyone walking alongside. When Skye puts the horse on a lunge line, Katie can ride in a big circle on her own. Skye, Katie, and Boomer make a great team!"

"This horse business is all new to me. What's a lunge line?" Mrs. Thomas sounded genuinely interested.

At last, Katie spoke in a decent tone. "It's kinda like a long rope that Skye ties on the horse. When it's hooked to his bridle, Boomer walks in circles while Skye guides him from the center of the corral. That way I don't have to worry about riding him off a cliff or something." She reached for her glass and finished her drink.

"You don't know how happy I am to hear how well this is going," Mrs. Thomas said to Mrs. Chambers. "Even though Keith and I have our differences, we both have been worried about Katie. Ever since the accident, she's been holed up in her room."

"Well, what else is there to do?" Katie sassed.

Again, Skye's glance darted to Mrs. Chambers to watch her reaction. Mrs. Chambers kept her eyes on Mrs. Thomas.

"Now, don't get me wrong," Mrs. Thomas continued. "I'm thankful that we qualified to get all those electronics through state grants. But face it, Katie, you have no life outside your bedroom."

"Well, duh, Mother! None of my friends come around anymore. It's kinda hard to have a party if I'm the only one who shows up."

Mrs. Chambers rose and got a large baking dish and four dessert plates from the counter behind her. "Anyone for peach cobbler?"

Everyone was.

"Katie, don't you think that's changed since you've come here?" Mrs. Chambers made her point clear. "You seem to hit it off pretty well with our girls."

"Sure," Katie's voice filled with sarcasm, "but I can't exactly take them home to Jersey with me."

Wow! Skye peaked her eyebrows again. *Smartin' off to Mom Chambers too. Trouble.*

"Katie, that's not a polite way to answer Mrs. Chambers. Please say you're sorry."

No answer from Katie.

Mrs. Chambers started to serve the desserts. "Perhaps we can work on Katie's respect for elders while she's here as well as her horseback riding skills," she said firmly.

"Skye," Mrs. Thomas said, "your mom tells me you've been a foster child. How many different homes have you lived in?"

"Oh, about a dozen," Skye said. She dug her spoon into the dessert and took a big bite. Peach cobbler put a better taste in her mouth than the subject she knew was coming.

"That must have been difficult for you." Mrs. Thomas took her dessert from Mrs. Chambers. "But you seem to have adjusted well."

"Well, I gotta tell you," Skye said, "I was a mess. I hated everybody. Before I came here, I had run away a bunch of times. I was headed for jail."

"Oh, my." Mrs. Thomas' raised eyebrows gave away her every thought.

Mrs. Chambers couldn't resist putting in a word. "We got her just in time, Christine. I should say, 'The Lord got her just in time.' "

Skye beamed from ear to ear. "When I accepted Christ, my whole life changed. Thanks to him and Mom and Dad, I finally got my act together."

"She doesn't know where her real mom and dad are. I should be so lucky," Katie's full mouth mumbled.

Skye observed Mrs. Chambers' face twist into an obvious display of displeasure.

"Katie ..." Mrs. Thomas reprimanded lightly, then glanced at Skye. "So, are you involved in any other activities besides horses?"

"Yep," Skye answered. "I have a lot of things to keep me busy."

Mrs. Chambers worked on her dessert and coffee. Her blue eyes sparkled at Skye. "Skye is quite active. She gets good grades, she's the manager of the girls' softball team, and just recently she started taking violin lessons. Oh, and you should see her attack those computer games!"

Everyone laughed but Katie, who had stopped eating, her face red with anger.

"It sure sounds like this place helped you find yourself," Mrs. Thomas said to Skye. "That's what I've been praying will happen with Katie. She needs a goal, a purpose in life. Maybe Keystone Stables, and you folks, can help her find one."

In a flash, Katie was out of her seat, almost knocking it over. Her face flushed even redder. "But Skye's not blind!" Pushing away from the table, she grabbed her cane and made her way past her mother. Her audience sat stunned as Katie swept her cane and rushed out of the dining room. Finding her way down the hall, she turned into her bedroom. When she slammed the door, the whole house shook.

chapter six

Skye, glued to her chair, glanced at the two women at opposite ends of the table. Standing, Mrs. Thomas hastily wiped her mouth with the napkin. "I'm so sorry. I'll get her to apologize."

Mrs. Chambers raised her hand. "Wait, Christine. There's enough time for that." She looked at Skye. "Honey, would you please try to talk to her? No one can truly know how she feels, but maybe she'll listen to you. Go on. We'll wait here."

Mrs. Thomas edged back into her seat, stress draping her face like a mask.

"Sure, Mom," Skye said. "I can only try."

Biding her time, Skye laid her napkin down. She stood, and for the company's sake, forced a smile. *God, you're gonna have to help me with this one.* She prayed all the way down the hall.

"Just try to get her calmed down so we can talk!" Mrs. Chambers called after her.

Skye gave Mrs. Chambers a thumbs-up sign. She knocked softly on the door.

"Go away!" Katie yelled.

"Katie, it's me," Skye said. "I wanna talk to you."

"There's nothing to talk about. Just leave me alone."

"Well, you can't stay in there forever! Your peach cobbler is getting moldy. C'mon, let me in."

Silence.

"I'm not leaving!" Skye's tone made that clear.

Silence.

"Oh, all right!" Katie finally gave in.

Skye walked in and stood beside the open door.

Katie busied herself with a gadget and a bag of potato chips at her computer desk. She had already slipped on earphones.

"C'mon, Katie, let's have it," Skye said sharply. "What's with you? You are one nasty critter when your mother's around."

Katie backed up and flopped on the bed, sitting against the headboard. She clicked a tab on her book port and adjusted her earphones. "Hey, I'm busy, okay?" She scowled. "Later."

"I'm not leaving!" Skye practically bellowed. "So you might as well just make up your mind to talk." She walked over and sat on the foot of the bed.

In an instant, Katie's face shriveled up like an old prune. Laying down the device, she peeled off the earphones, her green eyes searching their black, empty world. "Skye, I don't need you. I don't need anybody. Don't you get it?"

"Hey, people care about you and what happens to you," Skye said. "Don't you get it?"

"Yeah, right," Katie snapped. "Like all my good friends. Where are they now?"

Skye's voice relaxed. "Probably running the other direction when you're around. You're not exactly Miss Congeniality. You're more like Miss Sourpuss."

"Skye, you—are—not—blind!" Katie poured out all her hurt and anger in five words.

"So I've heard," Skye said nonchalantly.

"And I am!" Katie sassed back.

"So what are you gonna do about it?"

"What?" Katie's voice squeaked.

"You heard me. What are you gonna do about it?"

Silence.

Skye's voice reflected deep concern. "This is one time you are not gonna hear someone say, 'I know how you feel,' because I don't. But you could make life a lot easier—and happier—for yourself."

"Why should I even bother?"

"I realize that your friends all have their own lives. And your life is a one-eighty since your accident. But, Katie, nobody wants to be around an old grump, blind or not."

"Easy for you to say."

"You know, your mother is right about your needing some kind of goal in your life. With all this stuff you have, you could be an A student again."

"I have goals," Katie smarted off.

"What are they?"

"To get up every morning."

Skye snickered. "Wow, what a life! C'mon, Katie. You can't stay hidden in your bedroom forever. There are lots of things blind people can do."

Katie snickered back. "Like what? Count beads?"

"Now, you know better than that. I've seen blind people on TV who work in offices and factories."

"Whoopee," Katie said and sneered.

"I've seen others do volunteer work at hospitals, even play instruments. Hey, I saw a TV program once about a blind girl who rode a horse in a show. She won a ribbon! What do you think of that?"

Silence.

"The way I see it, your parents—well, your mom for sure and probably your dad too—they want the best for you. That's why you're at Keystone Stables."

"If my parents wanted the best for me, they wouldn't be getting divorced. I hate them for that."

"Are you sure that's the reason? I think you're just being selfish."

"What do you mean?" Katie asked.

"Your mom says that when you three are together, all you do is argue over whose fault the accident was. How did it happen, Katie?"

"I don't wanna talk about it!"

"Why not?"

"It's over. It's in the past. I can't do anything about it. Okay?"

"It doesn't seem to be over at all, Katie, especially not in your head."

Katie pulled her legs tight against her chest and wrapped her arms around them. "Now you're gonna tell me what I'm thinking?"

Skye chose her next words carefully. "I know how I was thinking, a few years back. I was mad at the whole world. In some really awful foster homes, I felt just like a slave. I hated my foster parents, and they hated me. Some of them were only in it for the money."

"So ...?"

"So ... I was mad at everyone and everything; I couldn't think straight. I even hated God because he let it happen."

Silence.

"Katie, how did the accident happen?"

Katie lowered her head onto her knees. "Dad was driving," she said in a near whisper.

"And ...?"

The question hung heavily in the air.

Katie felt her way to the edge of the bed. Now sitting next to Skye, she stared straight ahead as though watching her past unfolding on a huge screen. "It was in the winter on a Saturday afternoon, and it was snowing buckets.

We were going to Aunt Carol's birthday party. Dad didn't want to go, but Mom insisted. On the way, they were arguing about something, and we slid on ice. Our car went sideways into another car. Mom and Dad were banged up a bit. The side where I was sitting got the worst of it. But it still wasn't as bad as the other car." She sighed. "I'll never forget the look of horror on the other driver's face as we hit him. He was killed. And that's the last thing I ever saw."

"Oh, Katie, how awful!" Skye said.

"I was in the hospital and rehab for months. At first, Mom and Dad were there for me, but after a while, all they did was blame each other and fight. Sometimes their fights were over really stupid things."

"And you blame both of them, don't you?"

Silence.

"Katie?"

"Well, why shouldn't I?" Her voice took on a hurt tone again. "And now the divorce is making it a thousand times worse."

Skye positioned herself on the bed right next to Katie. "Can't you see that they're already on a big guilt trip without your reminding them every day?"

"No, I can't see!" Katie's sarcasm sliced the air like a sharp knife.

Skye pleaded her case. "Nothing changed in my life until I faced myself and the fact that I was mean and hateful, not because of anyone else but because of my own attitude. Katie, have you thought about asking God to forgive you for your rotten attitude? And shouldn't you forgive your parents?"

"Right now I don't think God cares about me at all." Katie sniffled.

Skye glanced at Katie, whose tears trickled down bright red cheeks.

"That's how I felt about God too," Skye said softly. "But he does care, more than we'll ever know. It took me a while, but when I realized that, things started turning around—for the better. Why don't you try it?"

Katie sat on the edge of the bed, tears flowing, nose sniffling.

Skye spotted a box of tissues, grabbed a handful, and passed them to Katie. "Here, looks like you could use some of these."

Katie wiped her cheeks and blew her nose. "Gosh, I never thought any of this could be my own fault."

"If your parents see that you have come to grips with your blindness and you've set some goals, maybe, just maybe, they'll try to work their differences out. You could make it a lot easier for them."

"What should I do, Skye?"

"Let's pray. You can ask the Lord to forgive you. I'll help you, okay?"

"Okay." Katie sniffled.

Skye started, "Dear God, here's my new friend Katie, who could really use your help. Go ahead, Katie ..."

Skye listened while Katie poured her heart out. She asked God to change her from the inside out. When they had finished, Katie let out a long sigh of relief. Her face seemed to glow, Skye thought, with a smile from deep down in her heart.

Katie wiped her nose, adding the tissue to a pile of wet balls already dotting the bed. She reached and touched Skye's arm. "Thanks."

"No problem," Skye replied. "Only God can make you feel that clean."

Katie paused and then said, "Skye, I sure wish I knew what you looked like."

"I'm just an ordinary kid, Katie," Skye said.

"Skye ..." Katie hesitated. "Will you let me touch your face? I'd like to know what my new best friend looks like."

Skye paused. "Um ... sure."

"I just want you to know I don't go around feeling people's faces all the time." Katie snickered. "But I'd really like to."

"Sure." Skye turned as Katie lifted her hands. Closing her eyes, Skye imagined again what blindness would really be like.

Gently, Katie's fingers felt Skye's long, silky hair. She felt her forehead, fingering her eyebrows and curly eyelashes, her cheeks and button nose, finally her lips drawn into a big smile. Then Skye looked at Katie, whose face now radiated with her own warm smile.

"Gosh, you're pretty," Katie said.

"Only a blind person would tell me that," Skye said.

Both girls burst into laughter, the tension between them dissolving instantly.

"Well, you're still one of my favoritist people in the whole wide world!" Katie added. She then seemed to focus beyond Skye, her beautiful green eyes darting as if to follow a distant, elusive dream.

"Skye, you said before that you had seen a blind girl ride in a horse show."

"Right on," Skye said. "Why?"

Katie stood, her face set in determination. "Skye, I want to barrel race a horse!"

chapter seven

Well, it is possible!" Mrs. Chambers said. Sitting on Boomer, she pushed her suede Stetson back on her head and patted the Pinto's neck. He oozed a white lather of sweat and huffed like a locomotive. "With a horse trained like this little guy, I think Katie can do it."

Skye shielded her eyes from the morning sun as she and Katie leaned against the fence of the Keystone Stables practice field. "You mean it, Mom?" Skye said.

"No kidding?" Katie's excitement burst through a mouthful of bubblegum.

"Ride 'em, cowgirl!" Mr. Chambers shouted from the small paddock where he, Morgan, and Chad instructed the other students.

"Looks like another blue ribbon for you and Boomer in the horse show, Mrs. C.!" Chad yelled.

Mrs. Chambers waved toward the paddock and smiled. She turned her attention back to the girls. "Katie, it'll take a lot of hard work, but after watching you ride Boomer for just a few weeks, I think you two can do it."

"How'd it feel running the barrels with your eyes closed?" Skye asked.

"Needless to say, quite different," Mrs. Chambers answered. "It forced me to rely much more on my instincts—and Boomer's. He knows the routine like he was born in a barrel."

They all laughed.

"Katie," Mrs. Chambers continued, "the first thing you'll have to do is learn the cloverleaf layout of the three barrels. Once you memorize the course and the distance between the barrels, you can learn how to sense when Boomer's ready to cut, either to the left or right. You already have excellent balance, so timing is your key to success here."

"How far apart are the barrels?" Katie asked.

"Oh," Mrs. Chambers answered, "in a standard course, the barrels are about a hundred feet apart. In kids' terms, that's about a third of a football field."

"I'm no barrel racer, but can I help?" Skye asked.

"You sure may," Mrs. Chambers said. "You and Katie can ride double and walk Boomer in the cloverleaf pattern over and over. Then you can graduate to a trot. When Katie feels confident, she can try it herself. Eventually we'll move on to the faster pace. Katie can ride with me until she learns the feel of the run."

"How long does it take to race the three barrels?" Katie asked.

"The best riders can do it in about fifteen seconds," Skye said. "But since you're a kid, and you'll be in a special-needs class, I'd say thirty seconds would be good, right, Mom?"

"That's probably a good guess." Mrs. Chambers dismounted and offered Boomer's reins to Skye.

Skye squeezed between the fence railings, took the reins, and petted Boomer's muzzle.

"What happens if a rider or a horse hits a barrel?" Katie asked.

"If you just brush against it," Mrs. Chambers said, "you aren't penalized, but it does slow the horse down a little."

"The worst thing that can happen is knocking over a barrel," Skye added. "You get five seconds slapped onto your total time. You get docked some points for losing your hat too!"

"And there goes your chance of winning a ribbon or placing at all," Mrs. Chambers said.

"Wow. I'm ready to start," Katie said. "I can't wait!"

"You girls can start anytime," Mrs. Chambers said as she slipped through the fence railings and pointed toward two objects lying on the lawn behind the girls. "I see your helmets are ready for you to get started."

"What's wrong with right now?" Skye asked.

"Yeah." Katie's voice bubbled. "How about right now?"

"Go for it!" Mrs. Chambers said. "If you need me, I'll be helping Joey with his first lesson in hoof cleaning."

"Okay, Mom." Skye turned to Katie. "I think the best way to do this is for you to sit in the saddle. I'll mount in back of you. I'll tell you when Boomer approaches a barrel."

"That'll work," Katie said.

Helmets in place, the girls mounted the horse and started their practice. For an hour, they simply walked through the cloverleaf pattern of barrels. Boomer led as though he were an electric horse on a track.

"Just remember," Skye explained as they rounded a barrel, "if your first turn is clockwise, then the next two must be counterclockwise. Boomer knows this. See how he starts to cut even before you rein him?"

"Yeah, I can sense that in the way his body moves. This is too cool."

"And remember to let him have his head as he's coming out of the cut. You just hang on to the horn and press your legs into his sides. That'll tell him that you're ready for the next barrel. After you round the third one, you race for the finish line like his tail's on fire. He can really move."

Both girls giggled.

"When do you think we'll be ready to trot and run?" Katie asked.

"Mom and Dad will have to decide that, but I think in a few weeks you'll be ready for Mom to work with you. Let's do one more run, and we'll call it quits for the day. Okay?"

"Okay," Katie said.

The team walked through two-thirds of the course before anyone spoke. Skye's attention wandered to the paddock where Chad was busy with his students.

"I've been thinking ..." Katie said.

"Oh ... about what?" Skye came back from her daydream.

"The horse show's at the end of the summer, isn't it?"

"Yeah, it's the third week in August. It starts the twenty-third or something like that. Why?"

Katie paused before answering.

"Do you have something up your sleeve?" Skye asked.

"My birthday is the twenty-first."

"And?"

"Do you know what I want more than anything else in the world?"

"To be able to see," Skye said emphatically.

"No—well—besides that."

"I give up. What?"

"I want my parents to get back together. Don't you remember our talk the other day?"

"Oh, right. So what does the horse show have to do with your parents? Or your birthday?"

"Well, when we talked, you said I needed a goal, something to show my parents that I'm getting on with life."

"And so here we are, on Boomer's back, goin' in circles."

The girls giggled again.

"I wanna barrel race in that horse show, Skye."

Skye swallowed hard. "Gosh, I don't know, Katie. That's only two months of practice time. Are you— "

"Listen, Skye." Katie's tone was as determined as ever. "I know I can do this, especially if I know my parents are coming to see me."

"Well, how will you get them here? And at the same time?"

"For my birthday!" Katie's excitement was obvious. "I know they'll both come for that, and then they can stay for the horse show, and they can see me ride this super horse, and— "

"Whoa, Boomer!" Skye said as the girls rode the horse across the finish line. "And whoa, Katie! That's expecting an awful lot of yourself and your parents in such a short time."

Skye slid off the horse, and Katie followed. The girls led Boomer to the barn.

"I can do this," Katie said, smacking her gum. "If I win the blue ribbon, they'll get back together. I just know it."

"Well, let's discuss your plan with Mom and Dad first. And maybe we should all pray about it." Skye had exhausted her arguments.

"You pray about it," Katie said. "I'll just do it!"

The next few weeks found Skye and Katie practicing barrel racing every chance they had. Katie progressed so well that Mrs. Chambers started working the routine with her. Together they rode Boomer in a slow canter.

By the end of July, Mrs. Chambers agreed that Katie was ready to run the course by herself. Despite Katie's pudginess, her natural riding ability impressed everyone. She credited her skill to her younger years of cheerleading and sports. Most impressive, though, was her new attitude. Casting Skye's caution to the wind, she believed that her family's future depended on her winning a blue ribbon at the horse show. Katie had something to prove!

Skye and Katie were becoming the best of friends, sharing their hopes and dreams. Of all the things they loved to discuss, horses topped the list. But Skye had little success convincing Katie to trust more in God. She couldn't even get her new friend to church or to youth activities.

Through the month of July, Katie's parents visited only twice, at different times. Mrs. Thomas came on her weekdays off from work. Mr. Thomas came on weekends. Skye wondered if he were intentionally avoiding his wife. Caught in the middle, Katie tried to be upbeat, showing the "new" her to everyone around.

Now, the last Saturday in July, Mr. Thomas was visiting again, and Mr. Chambers suggested a trail ride to take advantage of the beautiful warm day. On a dirt road winding through the backwoods of Keystone, Mr. Chambers and Mr. Thomas led the way on their horses. Skye and Katie followed close behind on Champ and Boomer. Katie fed her mouth a steady flow of candy from a stash in her shirt pocket.

Skye leaned forward and stroked Champ's silky mane. "Katie, we're going through some thick woods now. You should see how green everything is."

"Sh-h," Katie whispered. "I wanna hear what they're talking about." She pointed forward. "And, Skye, I can feel that we're in the woods. It's much cooler in the shade."

"So, Keith, how long since you've been on a horse?" Mr. Chambers asked.

"It's been years." Mr. Thomas' chubby hand rubbed through a head of straight blond hair. "I had forgotten how great riding is. I grew up in the country. I always had a pet pony or some grade horse my dad had picked up at auction. But after Katie's mother and I were married, we moved to the city where there were more job opportunities."

"You're in sales?" Mr. Chambers asked.

"Yes. Books. Wholesale. Right now, I'm trying to get a distribution business started online. If I can make it work from a home office, I'd like to move back to the country."

Mr. Chambers squared his Stetson. "Going into my own computer business was the best career decision I ever made. I had no idea that the Lord had this kids' ministry in mind for Eileen and me. Buying Keystone opened up a whole new world for both of us."

"I'd really like to be out in the wide-open spaces again." Mr. Thomas shot a quick glance back at his daughter. "And the way Katie has taken to riding, maybe we could look into getting a horse for her."

"We, Dad?" Katie was all ears. "You mean you and Mom?"

"No, I should have said 'I,' not 'we.' Nice try, Katie, but your mother and I have too many differences to get back together right now." Mr. Thomas punched his thumb over his shoulder. "You'd think there's nothing else to talk about but her mother and me. Katie sounds like her replay button is stuck."

"I don't know many kids who are glad about their parents' divorce," Mr. Chambers said. "It's important to try to understand their viewpoint."

"I thought she'd be glad we split up." Mr. Thomas spoke as if Katie were miles away. "All we did was fight. Katie even told her mother and me that she hated us. Now, that's hard to swallow from your own kid. I just couldn't cope anymore."

"Dad, I don't hate you," Katie interjected. "I didn't mean that at all."

"Well, you could've fooled me. It sure sounded like it," Mr. Thomas said. "A few times I thought the three of us were headed for a knock-down drag-out fight. Wrestlemania at the Thomas house!"

"Mr. Thomas?" Skye could keep quiet no longer.

"Hello!" he answered.

"Could I say something?"

"You're on," he said.

"I think I know a little bit how Katie feels," Skye said. "Life can really be screwed up and all, but a kid still loves her parents—deep down."

"Some kids sure have a funny way of showing it." Mr. Thomas glanced back and scowled at his daughter.

Mr. Chambers pointed to his right and deliberately changed the subject. "Let's take this trail that follows the stream. It leads through a huge cluster of pines to the back line of our property. Then we can swing around to another dirt road. That'll bring us to the pasture and pond right behind the barn."

The group headed off the road. Single file, each horse and rider took the narrow path into deeper woods that melded into a forest of towering pines. After a short distance on the new trail, the riders dismounted, allowing the horses to sip from the gurgling brook. Trying to ignore the tension between Katie and her dad, Skye basked in the beauty of the woods, the feel of the ride, the awesome smells of the horses and pine trees.

"It doesn't get any better than this, does it, Katie?" Skye said as they all mounted and started through the woods again.

"It would be if Mom were here!" Katie said loud enough for her father to hear.

"Duh," Skye whispered. "Just cool it! You do sound like your replay button is stuck!"

"Katie, need I remind you that your mother hates horses?" Mr. Thomas' tone sounded mocking. "By the way, I thought you did too."

"Katie doesn't hate them," Skye informed the man. "She loves them, especially Boomer."

The riders reined their horses out of the pines and onto a dirt road.

Besides a pocketful of candy, Katie focused on convincing her dad that all was not lost. "Dad, remember how I said I hated everything?"

"How could I forget?" Mr. Thomas said. "Four years of nothing but 'I hate this; I hate that; I hate you.' "

"She didn't mean it," Skye said.

"Well, maybe I did hate some things, but it was because of my blindness, Dad. That's why I want you to see that I've changed. I don't hate everything. Skye and Mr. and Mrs. C. have shown me that I need goals. And now I have some."

"Hmm," Mr. Thomas said. "Well, I have to hand it to you. You did surprise me by riding that horse."

"Dad," Katie rushed her words, "do you remember what next month is?"

"August!" he said without hesitation.

"What's in August?" Katie asked.

Mr. Thomas scratched the back of his neck. "Well, I know school usually starts. Am I missing something here?"

"It's my birthday!" Katie informed him.

"Oh, that's right," Mr. Thomas said. "You know I'm terrible with dates."

"And there's a horse show!" Skye couldn't resist putting her two cents' worth in.

Katie placed her index finger to her lips. "Sh-h," she said.

"What's the matter with you?" Skye whispered and shrugged her shoulders.

"Just sh-h," Katie repeated.

"We always make a big deal of birthdays at Keystone." Mr. Chambers chuckled. "Whether you're fourteen or forty, we do it up right!"

"Yeah," Skye said. "We'll probably have a big party with balloons and cake and everything!"

"I hope the cake is chocolate. Dad, can you come for my birthday?" Katie pressed her father.

Without missing a beat, Mr. Thomas asked, "Will your mother be here?"

"Probably not," Katie answered coolly.

Now how does she know that? Skye reasoned. *She didn't even ask her yet.*

"And what about the horse show?" Mr. Thomas asked.

"Katie's been—" Mr. Chambers started.

"It's a secret," Katie interrupted, "but I might have a big surprise."

"You mean you might be riding in the horse show?" Mr. Thomas asked.

"She and Boomer..." Skye almost gave it away. "Oops, sorry!"

"It's a secret!" Katie interrupted again with a more pointed tone. "Will you come? My birthday is just two days before the show. You could stay for both."

"Well, I can't make any promises," Mr. Thomas said, "but I'll check my schedule."

"I think you'd really enjoy the show," Mr. Chambers said. "It's the big event of the year in Snyder County. I hope you can make it."

"Is it on a weekend?" Mr. Thomas asked.

"Yes," Mr. Chambers answered. "It's always held the last Saturday in August."

"Well, we'll see," Mr. Thomas said.

"Dad, please!" Katie pleaded.

"Katie, that's the best I can do. We'll see." Mr. Thomas' response was stern this time.

The group followed the dirt road that led to a fenced pasture.

"Everyone, stop here." Mr. Chambers dismounted. "I'll swing the gate open. We'll ride to the barn by encircling the pond. It's a little shorter than taking the road."

The group waited while Mr. Chambers unlatched the gate. He swung it open, and Mr. Thomas rode through, followed by Katie. Skye brought up the rear, leading Mr. Chambers' horse.

In seconds, every horse had succumbed to the lure of the succulent grass. Like nails to a magnet, their heads were drawn to the ground. In greedy snatches, they grabbed and nibbled, trying to catch a quick meal while Mr. Chambers secured the gate.

"Skye," Katie whispered, "where's the barn?"

"It's about a hundred yards straight ahead," Skye said. "But the pond is — "

"I'm gonna show Dad how much I've learned." Katie pulled up Boomer's head and kicked him in the belly. "Watch!"

In an accelerating trot, Boomer started running through the field, straight toward the water.

"Hey, Dad," Katie yelled. "Watch how good I can ride!"

"Katie, get back here!" her dad yelled. "You're heading— "

"Boomer knows the way to the barn!" Katie yelled back.

"You're heading right toward the pond!" Mr. Chambers shouted and took a running leap unto his horse.

"Katie! Cut him to the left! Katie!" Skye screamed.

chapter nine

"Whoa, Boomer!" Katie screamed. She yanked the reins to her left. In a hoofbeat, the champion barrel racer cut sharply in that direction.

Boomer went one way, and Katie went another. She flew off the horse's back and plunged into the pond with the biggest belly flop Skye had ever seen.

Splash! Water exploded like a mushroom cloud. Weeds and mud flew everywhere.

"Katie!" everyone yelled at once.

Mr. Chambers kicked his horse into high gear toward the pond. Close behind rode Skye and Mr. Thomas.

Katie's chubby arms and legs flailed like mini paddle wheels. More water, weeds, and mud flew. Somehow, in seconds, she managed to turn herself around. She sputtered and gagged, trying desperately to regain her balance on a bed of slippery stones.

Splash!

Back she flopped, fighting the waist-high water that forced her into an unwanted sit.

"Don't move!" Mr. Chambers yelled.

"C'mon, Champ." Skye urged her horse into a full gallop.

"We're coming!" Mr. Thomas' voice had risen an octave.

"I'm okay." With both hands, Katie fought clinging hair, weeds, and mud, wiping them away from her face. "I'm okay, I said."

Paying no heed, three anxious riders and their horses galloped full speed ahead.

Again, Katie tried to stand.

Splash!

This time, only the girl's head and shoulders remained above the water. "Oh, I give up!" she shrieked.

Suddenly, as though an invisible feather had teased her nose, Katie started to giggle. By the time the horses slid to a stop, she was laughing like a drenched hyena.

"Katie, I'm here!" Mr. Chambers jumped from his horse, ran into the water, and led the girl out.

Skye and Mr. Thomas made quick work of dismounting.

"Does anything hurt?" Mr. Thomas asked.

"N—No!" Doubled over in laughter, Katie forced her words out. "Just my sides—from laughing."

"That was pretty dumb." Skye's fear suddenly dissolved. "And what's so funny?"

"I—I'm okay ..." Katie could barely speak. "That—I guess that was my bath for today!"

Skye, now giggling herself, pulled muddy clumps away from both sides of Katie's headgear. "You look ridiculous! Pond grass is sticking out from under your helmet. You look like one of Mom's potted plants."

"You do look kind of funny." Relieved, Mr. Thomas snickered. "I'm sure glad you were wearing that helmet."

"But helmets only protect heads, not belly buttons!" Mr. Chambers' comment delivered the final verdict.

Peals of laughter exploded. Even Champ joined in with a whinny.

Friday evening, while Mr. and Mrs. Chambers played table games with the boys in the dining room, Katie, Skye, and Morgan played Scrabble in Katie's bedroom. With the Braille board on the bed, they had almost finished their second game.

"Find an open *A* on the board, and I can make QUAIL," Katie said. She grabbed a handful of pretzel sticks from a bag and shoved them into her mouth.

"So that's where that nasty *Q*'s been hiding," Morgan said. "You had it all along."

"Yep." Katie's full cheeks smiled as she felt her small wooden tiles. "And I just got a *U*," she mumbled.

Skye studied the board and spotted an *A*. "Hey, there's one. Down in the lower left corner. You can place your word across. Wow, that's a triple word! You're gonna get mega points for that one!"

Katie fingered each letter near the corner of the board until she found the *A*. She placed two letters on each side of it. "That should be forty-five points, right?"

Skye handed the letter bag to Katie. "Morgan, me thinks we is getting skunked. And bad."

Morgan giggled. "We're gettin' beat up by a blind kid. We are in *big* trouble."

"You should see me bowl!" Katie joined in the giggles. "Mom took me once last summer, and I scored almost a hundred!"

Skye and Morgan raised their eyebrows and smiled.

"Hey, speaking of bowling," Morgan said, "our youth group is going sometime this month. You should go with us."

Skye placed four letters on the board and added her score. "Ten points. And speaking of the Youth for Truth group, our picnic is tomorrow afternoon back at Piney Hollow. Katie, you're coming, aren't you?"

"I sure hope so." Morgan took her turn and flipped her hair back. "You've never met all the neat kids at our church. Don't you think it's time?"

"How many are in the group?" Katie asked between more pretzel bites.

"Oh, about a dozen," Skye said. "And they're all cool."

"Listen, guys." Katie fingered her new letters. "I'm not really into things like that. After I went blind, the kids at my church didn't bother with me. Mom even took me to youth groups at three other churches, but I guess I cramped their style too. Nothing ever came of it. I'm still waiting for just one of those kids to call."

Skye pushed her long hair back off her face. "But our kids are different. Chad's in the group—and you already know him. Then there's Melissa, and Bobby, and—"

"I don't think so." Katie started in on another handful of pretzels.

"You've never really given them a chance." Morgan played three letters and added her score. "Fifteen points. Could I have a pretzel?"

"Hey, nobody wants to bother with a blind kid, okay?" Katie handed Morgan the bag. "I'll just stay here in my room with my stuff. I have lots to do. I wanna look up some things about horses on the Web. I'll be fine."

Skye noticed how fast the pretzels were going. "But Katie, we're gonna have all kinds of food." *That should get her attention.*

"How about potatoes baked on hot coals?" Morgan said between pretzel bites. "Or toasted marshmallows? Yum-my!"

"Hmm." Katie's face had a faraway look. "Nah, I guess not. I'll just grab something from the fridge here."

"Well, don't you want to be with Boomer?" Skye said, grabbing a pretzel and placing the bag out of Katie's reach. "If you don't ride him, someone else will. We'll be taking all six horses out."

"Yeah," Morgan said, "why don't you just go for his sake? He's used to you, not some crazy kids who'll kick him in the belly all afternoon."

"Hmm." Katie had that faraway look again. "How do all those kids ride only six horses?"

"They take turns going on short trail rides," Skye said. "Champ and I usually lead each group. If you go, you can help me. You can ride Boomer all afternoon. Hey, you could show everybody how to ride a horse around the pond!"

The girls laughed.

"Hmm." Katie drifted deep in thought. "I guess I could go, just for Boomer. Sounds like he needs me."

Skye and Morgan smiled and gave each other a thumbs-up.

As Skye had promised, she and Katie spent the afternoon taking four kids at a time on short trail rides around Piney Hollow. At the campsite, Mr. and Mrs. Chambers and Morgan entertained with ATV rides, bug and leaf hunts, and lessons about campfire cooking. Dozens of hot dogs, baked potatoes, and marshmallows later, the youth group encircled the campfire and sang choruses, with Chad accompanying on his guitar.

From the onset, the Youth for Truth teens welcomed Katie and Keystone's three other students. Immersed in the chitchat, Katie answered oodles of questions that expressed genuine interest in her, not only as a blind person but also as just another kid.

Giving Katie the space to make new friends, Skye and Morgan allowed themselves to be distracted, Skye mostly with Chad. During a short break before the evening devotional, Skye joined Katie, who sat facing the embers of the dying fire.

"So, Katie, how's it goin'?" Skye asked.

"That food was super!" Katie exclaimed. "When do we get to do this again? I had well—I won't tell you all I scarfed down, but that was great."

"Yeah, I just love campfire food," Skye agreed. "And how are you doin' with the kids?"

"I don't believe this," Katie answered. "Are they for real?"

"What do you mean?" Skye was hoping for a good report.

"I think they really like me."

Skye let out a long sigh. "Sure they like you. I told you they're a neat bunch of kids."

"Melissa told me how she met you at the Maranatha Treatment Center where you both were clients. She seems really cool."

"Yep, she is. We hang out together at school and church all the time."

"And who's this Bobby kid? He cracked me up."

"That's Bobby Noll." Skye chuckled. "He can be a real pain, but he's into music big-time. Did he tell you about his trumpet?"

Katie giggled. "That's all he talked about. He acts like the trumpet's his best friend. Speaking of music, Chad is awesome with that guitar."

Chad looks so dreamy tonight! Skye glanced toward a cluster of boys laughing near the chuck wagon. Chad stood in the middle. *He's probably telling his latest string of jokes*. "He just does everything so-o-o well." Skye sighed.

Katie giggled again. "Now how did I know you were gonna say that?"

Skye's face flushed hot. "Oh, never mind," she joked.

"Okay, kids!" Mr. Chambers' powerful voice commanded attention as he stood near the fire. "Gather around one last time. We're going to wrap up the day with devotions and testimonies, so think about what you'd like to say."

The campers quickly gathered, sitting on crates and buckets around the fire. Morgan parked her Jazzy next to Katie.

Skye glanced to the left of the chuck wagon where Champ stood lined up at a hitching post with the other horses. At a table in front of the wagon, Mrs. Chambers bustled about, finishing her supper chores.

"I sure hope he doesn't call on me." Katie's whisper drew Skye's attention back to the circle.

"Don't worry," Skye said as she eyed Chad directly across from her. "Saying anything is strictly voluntary."

"Phew-w-w." Katie let out a long sigh. "I don't exactly have anything to praise the Lord for anyway."

Mr. Chambers opened in prayer. After giving a devotional from the book of Psalms, he delivered a short challenge. "Would any of you want to tell what the Lord has done in your lives? You could be a great encouragement to the others. Anyone?"

With a warm smile, the man glanced at each teen. Finally, his stare settled on Skye. It burned a hole right through her.

Uh-oh. I don't like that look. Panic shot through her body like ice water, and her heart started racing. She gnawed her lip, her fingers running swiftly through her hair.

The Lord has been good, Skye told herself, *but I've never given a testimony in front of the whole world! And I don't plan to!* Her darting eyes found Bobby. *And at our last youth meeting, I told him to get lost. He'll think I'm a hypocrite!*

Skye scanned every face in the circle, her breath short and choppy. *Somebody say something! But not me!*

Seated next to Chad, Joey beamed a Cheshire grin from under his ten-gallon hat. An oversize tin sheriff's badge shone proudly from his western shirt. The beaming boy jumped up, charged toward Mr. Chambers, and wrapped him tightly with both arms. "Jesus loves you, Mr. C., and I do too."

Mr. Chambers folded his muscular arms around the boy. "And I love you, Joey."

Joey, still smiling broadly, dashed back to his seat and squared his hat just as he had seen Mr. Chambers do many times before.

A nervous silence settled over the campfire. The teens sat in their tight circle ... staring at the coals ... waiting ... as eager to say a word as the dying coals were willing to burn.

Mr. Chambers folded his arms and waited. "I'll give you a moment to think about what you'd like to say."

Finally, Chad raised his hand. "I'd like to say something."

"Go right ahead." Mr. Chambers grabbed at the chance to let someone else speak.

Chad stood, and his dimples highlighted a set of perfect teeth. "I just wanna say that the Lord has really been good to me. He allowed me to get two jobs this summer, one at the hardware store and one here at Keystone, helping kids learn to ride. All that money goes into my college fund. So I just wanna thank him." He sat and sent a special smile in Skye's direction.

Whoa! Skye's racing heart tore for the finish line, out of her chest and up her throat. *Chad, you are too cool.* Her face was anything but.

"Thanks," Mr. Chambers said. "Anyone else?"

With the wave of her hand, Morgan got the man's attention.

"You're on, young lady," he said.

Morgan took a deep breath and began. "Most of you know that I was born with cerebral palsy, and I've never been able to walk."

Everyone nodded.

"Well, for a long time I was really mad at God for letting me be born like this. There was a time when I thought I was useless. I didn't even want to live. No one in my family is a Christian, so we never went to church. But then I came here to Keystone Stables, and I learned that God has a special purpose for me. It was only after I accepted Christ that I could see that. I just wanna thank Mr. and Mrs. C.—and God—for showing me the right way."

"Thank you, Morgan." Mr. Chambers smiled again and ran his fingers down both sides of his mustache. "Sooner or later, we must all make the decision whether we want to turn it all over to God. Does anyone else have a testimony?"

Impulsive Bobby jumped up and poked his glasses back off the tip of his nose. "I wanna thank God for my trumpet!" He dropped back down abruptly, nearly overturning his bucket.

Peals of laughter erupted.

"And your father tells me he's thankful for earplugs!" Mr. Chambers chuckled. "I'm with him!"

More ripples of laughter.

Skye sat like a statue, her heart playing havoc in her chest.

But this was nothing new. Staring at Chad or being near him set her heart off like a flurry of butterflies or, worse, like a beating drum on the warpath. She could count on it!

Thumpity thump. Thumpity thump. Definitely not butterflies!

Skye had just about had enough. *Cut it out, heart!*

But wait.

Skye's thoughts had long since drifted away from Chad, back to the others and what they were saying. What was going on?

Thumpity thump. Thumpity thump. "It's your turn." Someone seemed to be speaking to Skye.

Skye looked at Mr. Chambers, whose eyes had already found hers. Their message was loud and clear.

Now, to make matters worse, busy Mrs. Chambers just happened to look toward Skye. "It's your turn!" That same voice spoke through the woman's beautiful blue eyes.

But I can't! More than ever, Skye wanted to crawl inside the crate on which she sat.

Thumpity thump. Chick-en ... Skye!

Am not ... am not ... am not!

"Anyone else before we close in prayer?" Mr. Chambers fired his question right at Skye.

Skye's glance swept the circle. Every pair of eyes, without exception, had found the same person.

Dad means me! Gulp!

Skye had been a Christian long enough to know that in times of crisis, the best thing to do was pray.

And the crisis is now! God, I need you. Right this minute. I do have a lot to thank you for. So if it is my turn, I'll do it!

Finally, Skye's chicken heart mustered a swell of new-found strength. Like an electric charge, courage coursed through every nerve in her body. In an instant, Skye the Coward became Skye the Brave!

She could do this.

She would do this—for her Lord.

Slowly, Skye stood.

Skye, go right ahead!" A smile of victory beamed from Mr. Chambers' face.

A circle of eyes riveted on Skye.

Mrs. Chambers strolled from her table and stood behind Joey. She folded her arms and gave Skye an assuring wink.

"I—I—"

"You can do this," a Voice whispered deep in Skye's soul.

Skye took a deep breath, determined.

Amazingly, words started flowing from her lips as fast as her heart was pounding. "I just wanna say that I used to be a pretty rotten kid. I blamed everybody else for all the trouble I caused. I ran away from everything and everybody, even God. But when Jesus came into my life, he gave me the guts to face my problems. I found out that it was him I was running away from all along. Now I know he's with me through anything. He's the best friend I have. That's all!" Skye looked at her foster mother for approval, released a deep, long sigh, and sank back down onto her crate.

Eyes watery, Mr. Chambers took a moment to find his voice. "Thank you, Skye. The Bible says that Christ wants to be as close as a brother to those who ask. If any of you would like to talk to me privately about your walk with God, see me afterward. Your testimonies were excellent. Let's stand and we'll close in prayer."

As Mr. Chambers started, Skye glanced at Morgan, who gave her a quick thumbs-up. Out of the corner of her eye, Skye watched Katie, who slowly stood with her head hung low. Her solemn face seemed set in stone.

Now what's goin' on in that brain of hers?

Skye just had to find out.

Sunday and time to go to church!

Katie surprised everyone. Dressed in her Sunday best, she arrived first at the breakfast table. She smiled all the way to church—and through it! It seemed to Skye that Katie actually listened to the video in teen class and to the pastor in the main service, as well. At dinner as at breakfast, Katie used her best manners, taking only one serving of every dish. Something was definitely different!

Skye studied her new friend as though Katie had grown an extra head. Despite prodding from Mr. and Mrs. Chambers as to why she had decided to attend church, Katie simply said, "I just wanted to. That's all." Not until the afternoon when the girls were grooming their horses in the barn did Skye have the chance to find out what was really going on.

"All right, Katie, let's have it," Skye said as she ran a metal comb through Champ's long, flowing tail.

"Have what? One of these brushes?" Katie's tone was light, almost a giggle. With a brush in each hand, she worked hard on Boomer's coat.

"You know perfectly well what. What's with you and church all of a sudden? And you usually inhale two plates of food at every meal. Are you sick or something?"

Silence filled the barn, except for two lazy horses whisking their tails to shoo away flies.

"Katie?"

"Oh, all right, Skye. You won't give up until I spill it. I want you to be the first to know. It's been killin' me to keep this in until you and I were alone."

"What? What?"

Katie rested her arms on Boomer's back, her eyes darting rapidly. "I've given everything to the Lord. I mean *everything*. I did it last night at the campfire."

"But I thought you did that in your bedroom a few weeks ago." Skye worked the comb through a stubborn knot in Champ's tail.

"Well, I only gave part of my life to God that day. Last night I gave up all the things I had been holding on to."

"What were you holdin' on to, and what made you give them up?"

"It was what the kids said. Mostly what you said, Skye."

"Me?" Skye's voice squeaked. "I hardly said anything. I just told the truth, the way the Lord has been helping me. It was tough to give that testimony, but now I'm glad I did it."

"Yeah, and remember what you said about running away from God?"

"How could I forget? I meant it."

"That's when I felt like somebody punched me right in the nose. I've been running away from God too, because I was mad at him. Just like you were."

"It's no fun runnin' from God, is it?" Skye asked. "You never get too far. I found that out the hard way."

"Me too," Katie said. "I realized last night that I had been runnin' from him not only with my attitude about blindness and my parents, but also about other things."

"Hmmm … let me guess. How about the way you eat all those bags of junk food and get no exercise? Then there's your attitude about schoolwork. Am I gettin' warm?"

"Right on." Katie resumed brushing Boomer's neck. "I realized last night that I've been using food as an out. Half the time I eat when I'm not even hungry! It just helps me get my mind off how frustrated and mad I am."

"Hey, you're not alone in that one. I used to do that with pills. Now, that was dumb with a capital *D*."

"Well, I really mean business this time," Katie said. "I want to come clean. I know if I do, my parents will get back together. Will you help me?"

"Well, sure." Skye jumped at the chance to help her new friend. "But what else can I do besides help you with Boomer?"

Katie slipped her arms around Boomer's neck and gave him a hug. He nickered.

"I have the Bible on cassette tapes buried under a pile of stuff here in my room."

"You do? Wow! That's awesome. I'd love to see it."

"My mother made me bring it. I also have a box full of Christian music CDs that I've kinda been ignoring. Actually, big-time ignoring. I want to start my life all over with God. But first, I need to houseclean my room. Will you help me?"

"Houseclean?"

"Let's go up to the house, and I'll show you."

The girls put their horses out to pasture and headed straight for Katie's room. In five minutes, they had dug out at least a dozen bags and boxes of snack foods that now lay in a foot-high pile on the bed.

"This answers a big question I've had since you got here." Skye flopped on the bed's small empty space next to the mound.

"What question?"

"I never could figure out why Mom and Dad allowed you to have all this stuff. They're into healthy eating big-time. I thought maybe your mom had made some kind of special deal with them or something."

"No special deal," Katie confessed.

"Mom and Dad don't know you have all this stuff, do they? How would they know? I mean, they don't spy on us or inspect our rooms."

Katie shrugged. "Mom told me they wouldn't allow me to have all this stuff in my room, so I lied to her. I said I'd give Mr. and Mrs. Chambers all of it to share with the other kids. As soon as Mom left, I hid it. Now I'm really sorry about lying to her and being so sneaky. You can have any of it that you want."

"Um, I'm not into junk food too much." Studying the pile, Skye spotted her favorite candy bar. "Although I do see something that definitely has my name on it."

"Help yourself!" Katie skirted the room's furnishings to reach her closet. There she felt for the handle, opened the door, and knelt down. "I almost forgot that I have a whole bunch of candy hidden in a shoe box." Reaching behind a row of shoes, she grabbed her prize stash and held it up. "See?"

"You are so ridiculous." Skye laughed. "Like you weren't gettin' enough to eat at the table!"

"I bet Joey and the other boys will love this." Katie hobbled on her knees to the bed and emptied the shoebox onto the pile. "I think that's all of it."

Skye stood and headed toward the door. "I'm gonna get Mom and an armful of plastic bags. She can figure out where to store this stuff."

"And who gets what—and when," Katie added.

"I'll be back in a minute!" Skye could hardly wait to seek out her mom and watch her reaction.

Katie sat on the only empty corner of the bed. "Then I want you to help me with one more project, okay?"

"What's that?" Skye stopped short at the doorway and looked back.

"Didn't you tell me when I first came that Mrs. Chambers has a treadmill somewhere?"

"Yep. She has it in the basement with some other exercise equipment."

"Don't you think I need to get in shape?" Katie giggled and pinched her sides. "If I lose some of these pounds, then my parents will know that I'm serious. Can you show me how to use that treadmill?"

"No problem," Skye said. "We can work out together. It wouldn't hurt me to do a little sweatin' either."

"Skye, hasn't anyone ever told you that horses sweat, boys perspire, but girls glisten?"

Skye laughed. "Then let's glisten and kiss those carbs good-bye!"

Happy birthday to you! Happy birthday to you! God bless you, dear Katie! Happy birthday to you!"

Laughter and popping balloons echoed through the Chambers' basement the last Thursday evening in August. Silly games and gifts in fancy paper took center stage while delicious smells of barbecue and freshly baked chocolate cake filled the air. Mr. Chambers was right. With the help of the youth group, Keystone Stables did birthdays up in a big way!

For weeks, Skye had helped Mr. and Mrs. Chambers and Morgan plan a "half surprise" for Katie. Katie knew about the party; she just didn't know about all the people who had been invited.

Despite the many church friends attending, Katie focused on one thing and one thing alone: her parents and whether both would be there. Had her scheme worked?

Arriving on Wednesday night, Mrs. Thomas had planned to stay for the party and the horse show, Katie's surprise debut!

Mr. Thomas, on the other hand, offered his daughter no satisfaction. "I'll try to make it," was all he would say whenever she called.

Thursday came. Katie put her father's arrival as the number one special event of the day, even ahead of her party. Whenever the phone rang or a car pulled in the driveway, Katie had only one response. "Is it Dad?"

But Thursday went by as quickly as it came. At nine o'clock the party ended, the guests all left, and Mr. Thomas still had not arrived.

In the basement, while Mrs. Chambers and Mrs. Thomas cleaned up the galley kitchen, the girls sat amid a sea of torn wrapping paper beside the Ping-Pong table. Katie slumped in her chair with her arms folded while Skye and Morgan inspected the beautiful and thoughtful gifts Katie had received. But Katie's mind was not on gifts.

Skye cuddled a large, brown teddy bear. "This is just about the cutest thing I've ever seen. He'll look super on your bed. His cool cowboy outfit matches the colors of your room. Didn't Chad give this to you?"

"Yes," Katie said glumly.

"And this Bible Library CD from Melissa has puzzles and quizzes on it." Morgan handed it to Katie. "It is so-o-o awesome!"

"Why didn't he come?" Katie fingered the case nonchalantly. Suddenly, streams of tears were making wet tracks down her fiery cheeks. "He didn't even call."

Ring-g-g!

"I'll get it!" Skye and the bear rushed to grab the phone off a nearby wall. "Hello, Chambers' residence. Skye speaking." Her eyes met Katie's, already turned toward the phone.

"Hello, Skye, this is Mr. Thomas. I'd like to speak to my daughter."

"Sure. She's right here. Just a sec." Skye handed Katie the phone and flopped the bear comfortably on her own lap.

"Who's on the phone, Skye?" Mrs. Chambers asked from the kitchen.

"It's Mr. Thomas," Skye yelled back, "for Katie."

"Hello, Dad?" A smile surfaced through Katie's tear-drenched face.

Chewing her lip, Skye exchanged glances with Morgan and gave the bear a hug.

"Yeah," Katie said flatly.

A long pause.

"But why not?" she whined. "But Da-a-a-ad! Don't you care about me?"

Morgan pursed her lips.

You're right. Skye shook her head. *This is so-o not good.*

"Yeah—sure—bye," Katie barely whispered.

Skye gently touched Katie's arm. "Here, I'll take the phone."

Katie choked back another flood of tears. "He said he doesn't think he can make the horse show. Something to do with his new business—or so he says."

Mrs. Thomas rushed in from the kitchen. A look of disgust settled over the woman's face as she sat down and stroked her daughter's long blonde hair. "I was afraid this would happen. He's always too busy!"

Katie faced her mother and shrugged, a clear signal to back off. "M-o-m ... don't," she said with a choking sob.

"Now don't let this spoil your birthday, Katie." Mrs. Thomas slowly pulled away. "Everyone's been so nice to you. And you've come so far in the few months you've been here." She looked at Skye. "Could you get us some tissues, please?"

"Yep. Be right back." Skye set the bear down, replaced the phone, and rushed into the kitchen. In seconds she returned and gave a handful of tissues to Katie. "Did you tell your mom how God's been helping you with Boomer? And with your weight?"

Mrs. Thomas smiled at Skye then studied her daughter. "I did notice you've trimmed down a little the last few weeks. You look great!"

Katie sat with her head down, tears dripping off her cheeks. She blew her nose.

Morgan offered encouraging words. "Mrs. Thomas, do you know she's been goin' to all our church services and youth activities too?"

"Yes. Every time she called, she gave me a full report." Mrs. Thomas smiled. "I'm so glad she's let God back into her life. I'm very proud of her."

"I wanna go to my room," Katie said, sobbing.

Mrs. Thomas gently touched her daughter's arm. "But Katie— "

"Mom, I just wanna go to my room!" she sassed. "Now!"

Whew ... nasty. Katie's demeanor took Skye aback.

"I guess the party's over," Morgan wisecracked.

She is so-o-o unreal. "I'll go with her," Skye's sharp tone betrayed her deepening anger with Katie.

Katie stood and again wiped her nose. "I don't care about anything," she smarted off. "Life stinks. And Skye, I know the way upstairs. You don't need to go with me."

"But I want to!" Skye insisted. *Maybe I can talk some sense into her.*

"I'll help clean up all this stuff." Morgan tried her best to lighten the mood that had soured the air like a backed-up drain. She scooped up paper balls from the floor, collecting them on her lap.

Mrs. Thomas released a long I-don't-know-what-to-do-next sigh. "Thanks, girls. Katie's fortunate to have two friends like you. Maybe all she needs is a good night's rest."

"No problem." Skye followed Katie toward the stairs.

"Good night, Katie," Mrs. Thomas said warmly. "I love you."

In mute defiance, Katie made her way up the staircase. Her silence said it all.

Friday, one day before the horse show!

A ham-and-egg breakfast at dawn started the hot summer day off right. Afterward, Keystone buzzed from the house to the barn to the field and back. There was so much to do: practicing events, polishing tack, grooming the horses until they glowed!

In the open field, Skye and Morgan worked Champ and Blaze through a tough obstacle course for their Advanced Trail classes. Mr. and Mrs. Chambers and Chad walked the three boys and their horses through the Beginners Showmanship routines in the small paddock. Between practices, Mrs. Chambers saw to it that each "cowpoke" had just the right western clothes, hat, boots, and all! Determined to have Keystone Stables come home with an armful of ribbons, everyone plunged in with both hands!

Everyone except Katie.

Katie, back to her old nasty self, kept busy with her mother—shopping and eating out. Returning after supper, she headed straight for her room.

The horse show? Only Skye's nagging convinced Katie to run Boomer through the course a few times and then groom him.

"I know what I'm doing," Katie bragged as she mounted Boomer, "and I don't need the practice."

"Listen, Katie, we *all* need it if we want to win," Skye said sharply as she checked Boomer's cinch. "And your attitude has you about one crummy millimeter away from Mom and Dad bootin' you out of the show!"

"I couldn't care less," Katie snapped as she took off toward the barrels. "Let them!"

While Skye finished last-minute barn chores on Friday night, her anger, frustration, and confusion just about finished her. She couldn't wait until family time in the living room after Katie and the three boys had gone to bed.

As Mr. Chambers read from the book of James, Skye stared at a framed picture of a white stallion. Struggling to listen, she found her thoughts wandering more than once … thinking about Champ … the horse show … Boomer and Katie.

Mr. Chambers continued, "This study in James … first chapter … wisdom … patience …"

Patience? Skye's attention swung back to Mr. Chambers. "Dad, how did you know I needed a lesson on patience? I'm going crazy with a certain person in this house," she confessed.

Mrs. Chambers gave Skye a compassionate smile. "Honey, we all know who you mean. Katie has tested everyone's patience."

Morgan played with a few fiery red strands. "I've been ready to pull my hair out more than once."

"Girls," Mr. Chambers said, "it's not an accident that this chapter in James talks about wisdom as well as patience. We need both of those traits in our own lives before we can even think about helping Katie."

Deep in thought, Skye stared at Mr. and Mrs. Chambers on the sofa. Morgan had parked her Jazzy beside them. Slumping back, Skye folded her arms and crossed her legs at the ankles. "I've just about given up. She is so-o-o frustrating. I feel like I'm on a roller coaster with her. One minute we're up; the next minute we're down. I don't know how to take her! She just makes me mad. That's all."

Mrs. Chambers spoke in a positive tone. "Girls, surely you remember how you tested our patience. And not too long ago at that, either. God can change anyone. Just give him time."

Mr. Chambers closed the Bible on his lap. "The best thing we can do for Katie is to love her through this crisis. I'm sure you girls know how parents can mess things up for teenagers." His mustache framed a teasing smile.

"Okay, okay," Skye conceded as she sat up straight. "I need to remind myself more often that God's always there for us. He's there for Katie too. Can we pray for her?"

"And her parents?" Morgan added.

"We sure can," Mrs. Chambers said. "Let's pray right now."

"And just be patient, girls." Mr. Chambers leaned forward and folded his hands. "God wants the Thomas family back together more than any of us do. Skye, why don't you start?"

"Okay, Dad." Skye closed her eyes. "Dear God, please help Katie ..."

Great job, Skye!" Mrs. Chambers' blue eyes sparkled with excitement as she stroked Champ's nose.

A radiant smile lit up Mr. Chambers' face. "All that practice paid off!" He nervously smoothed down his mustache. "Now that's what I call teamwork. Right, boys?" He glanced at Joey, Sam, and Leonard, who stood beside him, eyes wide with wonder.

"Whoa, way to go, Skye! That was one cool routine." Chad's dimples were nearly hidden in the shadow of his black hat as he patted Champ's sleek neck.

Morgan, mounted on Blaze, joined in congratulating Skye. "Our ribbons make a nice pair, Skye."

In her flashy western attire, Skye glowed with pride as she waved a first-place ribbon in her hand. "Yeah, red and blue do make a good match, don't they?"

Skye's suede Stetson, complete with hawk feather and leather braid, sat squarely on her head, leveled to her eyebrows. Her hair, drawn back into a bun, rested securely under the hat. A leather-fringed vest covered a blue-checkered shirt. A red necktie, cowhide gloves, blue jeans, chaps, and polished boots made Skye a perfect match for her mount.

Champ's bridle with blue browband set off a leather-cut saddle. The poncho roll highlighted his copper coat and silky mane and tail.

Cheers and applause exploded from a packed house in Snyder County's new indoor arena. Skye and Champ had just won the Junior Advanced Trail class!

"Thanks, guys! But Champ did it all. He was great!" Skye slid off her horse.

Chad took the prize from Skye's hand and held it up in front of the boys. "Okay, guys. See what you're shootin' for? You can do it too."

"And your classes are coming up soon," Mr. Chambers said to them. "We need to get you and your horses ready. C'mon." He turned to walk away.

"Okay, Mr. Chambers!" Joey trailed after the man. "I'm gonna win!"

"Me too," Sam said. He and Leonard followed Joey.

Mrs. Chambers gave Skye some last-minute instructions. "I'm going to help Morgan dismount; then I'll be busy with the boys. After you cool down Champ, would you help Katie get ready? Barrel racing is next."

"Yep," Skye answered. "I'll do my best to get her motivated. Where is she?"

Mrs. Chambers pointed to the nearest exit. "She's waiting out there in the hallway with Boomer. But she needs to be at the other end of the arena at the entrance gate when the barrel racing starts."

Skye glanced at her watch. "That's in about ten minutes. I'll have her there."

"Great," Mrs. Chambers said. "If you don't see us, we'll be with the boys at the horse trailer, going over last-minute details."

"I'll help get Katie ready," Chad said, stroking Champ's nose. "You know, Skye, sometime I'd like you to teach me that trail class routine. It looks like a lot of fun. Would you?"

Would I? Thumpity thump. Thumpity thump. Skye's heart was up to its old tricks. "I'd love to. You can even ride Champ. It's easy with a horse trained like him. Sure."

"Thanks. Maybe when I have a Saturday free?"

"Just call and let me know what time." Skye's face turned fiery hot. "I'll warn Champ to be on his best behavior." She tugged her horse's bridle. "C'mon, Champ."

With Chad by her side, Skye led the horse toward where Katie waited. "I sure wish she'd snap out of it," Skye said. "She's missin' a lot of fun."

"Yeah," Chad said. "Mr. C. told me what happened with her dad and all. It seems like she doesn't care whether she wins or loses today."

"She doesn't," Skye said, "but maybe you and I can— "

"Skye! Hello!" Amid the commotion, a voice yelled from somewhere to Skye's left. Stopping short, Skye scanned the boisterous crowd packed in a dozen rows of bleachers. "Chad, who's calling my name?"

Chad pushed his hat back and studied a sea of faces. "I don't know, but I heard it too."

"Skye! Chad! Over here!"

Chad pointed toward the main entrance. "Look, there in the doorway. It's Mrs. Thomas! Skye shifted her glance and saw Mrs. Thomas waving in the forefront of the bustling hallway of horses, contestants, and show attendees. "Hi, Mrs. Thomas!" Skye yelled as she and Chad waved back.

"We should tell her that Katie's event is next." Skye *click-click*ed her tongue, prompting Champ to follow.

"Skye," Chad said, grabbing Champ's bridle, "if you'd like, I can take Champ and cool him down while you talk to Mrs. Thomas. And don't worry about Katie. I'll get her and Boomer to their entrance gate."

Skye handed Chad the reins and started toward Mrs. Thomas. "Thanks. I'll see you after Katie's event."

Skye hurried to greet Mrs. Thomas. Just as she reached the doorway, Mr. Thomas came rushing to his wife's side.

Skye's face lit up with surprise. "Mr. Thomas, you're here!"

"Yes, we're here—together. I just parked the car—I think in the very last parking place in the lot," Mr. Thomas said with a chuckle.

Mrs. Thomas' smile now freed her face of the worry that had been her trademark. "I'm sorry we're late. Did we miss Katie's event?"

"Nope." Skye glanced at her watch and smiled back.

"I'm so glad we made it in time," Mr. Thomas said. "My business tied me up again, but that will be changing, thanks to you, Skye."

"Me? What did I do?"

Mr. Thomas looked affectionately at this wife. "Skye, you and Mr. and Mrs. Chambers—well, your entire Keystone Stables ministry—helped me realize what's really important in life. I've been doing a lot of serious thinking since I visited the ranch a few weeks ago. And with God's help, I'm getting my priorities in order. I know Katie and her mother need me now more than ever."

Skye beamed another broad smile. "Wow! That's the best news ever! I guess you know Katie's been a mess over what's happened with your family. We couldn't even convince her to do her best today. She didn't care about the show at all when she thought you weren't going to be here, Mr. Thomas."

"And I'm real sorry about that," the man said. "I only decided to come this morning after I prayed with our pastor. He also helped me see things more clearly."

"And when we get home, we'll be counseling with Reverend Kline on a regular basis." Mrs. Thomas' tone was filled with hope.

"Hey," Skye said, "we've got to let her know that you two are here—together."

"Attention, ladies and gentlemen," the loud speaker echoed. "The Special-Needs Barrel Racing starts in five minutes. We have six entries this year!"

Skye glanced at the other end of the arena where Katie would soon enter. "That's Katie's event. I don't have much time, but I think—"

"Barrel racing?" Mrs. Thomas seemed stunned. "All Katie ever told me was that she was riding in the show. But barrel racing? That sounds dangerous."

"Sounds like she's got something to prove," Mr. Thomas said as he touched Skye's shoulder. "Skye, don't worry about it. Let's surprise her."

"But ... she hasn't been practicing—"

"Sorry, folks." A man in a black uniform approached Skye, the Thomases, and a small crowd of onlookers now gawking in the doorway. "Unless you're waiting for a rider to come out, you need to move on. We gotta keep this open. There's lots of horse traffic coming through here."

The onlookers melded into the crowd, shuffling in all directions. Mr. and Mrs. Thomas started to walk away.

"Sir," Skye said to the security guard, "we *are* waiting for a rider."

"That's fine, but please step away from the doorway." The guard pointed inside the arena. "You can stand along the inside wall."

"Thank you," Skye said. She and the Thomases slipped inside, joining others who were waiting.

"Attention!" the loud speaker announced. "The first barrel racer is number twelve, Katie Thomas, on Boomer!"

Skye pointed to the center of the show ring. "Katie and Boomer are going to race around those three barrels full speed ahead. If they have the fastest time, they win!"

"Oh, my!" was all Mrs. Thomas could say.

At the other end of the arena, Chad led the Katie/Boomer team into the ring. A roar of applause shook the building.

"There she is!" Skye said. "See that thin wire stretched in front of Boomer? When he runs through that, the clock starts."

"I had no idea that's what she was up to," Mr. Thomas said. "Now that takes guts."

"Oh, my!" Mrs. Thomas' voice was high-pitched.

An anxious silence settled over the crowd. Every eye focused on the starting team as Chad led them to the starting wire and backed away.

Boomer was raring to go!

From her far corner of the arena, Skye watched as Katie fought to restrain the powerful animal. Neck arched and eyes wild, the horse's body tensed as he focused on the race before him. He tugged at the bit and pranced.

Katie tightened her hat string, took a deep breath, and kicked Boomer in the ribs.

The Pinto's ears pricked, every muscle tightened, and with one mighty surge, he lunged forward, tripping the wire. Off he went in a mad dash toward the barrels, just as he had trained to do so many times before.

"And they're off!" the loud speaker blared. The crowd went wild.

Skye glanced at the huge wall clock that ticked off each second.

"C'mon, Katie!" Mr. Thomas joined the screaming crowd. "You can do it!"

"Ride 'em, cowgirl!" Mrs. Thomas joined in.

Skye glanced from Katie, to the clock, back to Katie, whose sloppy riding around the first barrel was only too obvious to Skye.

Lean forward more! Skye wished she had a megaphone. *Your cut was too wide!*

Again, Skye glanced at the clock. Fifteen seconds. "Too slow," she said out loud.

The team rounded the second barrel. Out of the turn, Katie reined Boomer tight instead of giving him his head. He trotted to the third and final barrel.

Twenty-eight seconds, the clock flashed.

Katie, way too slow! You're blowin' it! Skye became more frustrated by the second!

"C'mon, Katie! Faster!" Mr. Thomas yelled.

"Go, Katie, go!" Mrs. Thomas' voice was getting hoarse.

A wider turn around the last barrel and off toward the finish line!

Now you can make up time! "Go! Go! Go!" Skye yelled.

Again, and for no clear reason, Katie held Boomer back.

Instead of running at top speed, the horse cantered. The team crossed the finish line like they were out for a Sunday afternoon ride.

Lazy applause matched Katie's sloppy effort.

"Thirty-four seconds," the loudspeaker announced. "There's lots of room here for you other riders. The blue ribbon is sayin', 'Come and git me!' "

"That time won't win a thing unless the other riders are on mules," Skye mumbled, but then she remembered Mr. Chambers' words. Wisdom. Patience.

Well, I'm glad she didn't get hurt, Skye told herself.

"Her heart just wasn't in it," Mr. Thomas said.

"Well, at least she didn't quit," Mrs. Thomas replied. "That's more than we've done lately."

Katie slowed Boomer to a walk as they left the ring and approached the exit door.

"I'll bring her out." Skye started toward Katie. "I have a feeling she'll be sorry she didn't do her best this time."

At the starting line, a new racing team approached the wire.

"Next contestant, number forty-three, Ian Weirick, on Cobalt!" echoed through the arena. Encouraging cheers erupted from the crowd.

Skye hurried to Boomer's side, grabbed his bridle, and touched the blind girl's arm. "It's me, Katie. I'll lead you out!" She had to bellow to make herself heard.

"Okay, Skye," Katie yelled and pushed her Stetson back. "At least I didn't lose my hat. That penalty would've been two seconds more. Not that it mattered!"

You weren't going fast enough to lose anything but the race! Skye bit her tongue before the words could fly out. "At least you finished the course, Katie, and you didn't get hurt. That's saying something."

In the hallway, Katie slid off a horse still raring to go. "Easy, Boomer."

"Thirty-four seconds is not exactly ribbon speed," Skye said as she grabbed Boomer's bridle to steady him. She glanced over her shoulder at the Thomases. Both held their index fingers to their lips. *Sh-h*, they mouthed silently.

"Yeah, I heard the man. No biggie," Katie snapped. Reaching toward the saddle, she hooked the stirrup over the horn and started to loosen the cinch. "Who was here to see me anyway?"

"Final time, twenty-seven seconds!" blared from the arena. "That puts Ian Weirick and Cobalt in first place!" Another round of applause split the air.

"I was here, Katie!" Mrs. Thomas tried to make herself heard over the din.

"Oh, hi, Mom," Katie replied without turning around. "Well, I'm glad you're here."

"And I'm here too." Mr. Thomas' voice cracked.

Katie stopped dead in her tracks.

Skye could only imagine what was going through the blind girl's mind.

Turning toward her father's voice, Katie glowed. "Dad!"

Mr. Thomas wrapped his arms around his daughter as though he hadn't seen her in years. "I'm so sorry, Katie. I'm so sorry." Eyes moist, the man waved his wife toward him.

"Oh, Dad," Katie said, "I'm sorry too, for not trying harder in the race. I want you to be proud of me."

"Katie," Mrs. Thomas cried, embracing the two, "we *are* proud of you, for what you've accomplished. And we have some good news for you. Your father and I are, well, we want to start over. With the Lord's help, we'll do it—together!"

"Oh, Mom," Katie said, her eyes watering. "I'm so glad!"

Skye stroked Boomer's chin, basking in the scene unfolding before her. "Wow! How cool, God," Skye whispered. "Thanks for answering prayer."

Katie gave a tender hug to her mom and dad then slowly turned. "Where's Skye?" she asked, wiping the tears from her face.

"Right here," Skye said.

Hand in hand, Mr. and Mrs. Thomas moved to the side.

Katie reached in Skye's direction. "I just wanna say thanks, Skye. Thanks for being my favoritist friend. You're the best!"

Skye took Katie's hand then slipped an arm around her shoulders. Her heart filled with the satisfaction and pride of a job well done, Skye now knew that God had used her for something very special.

She thought about the summer, an exciting summer that had taught her one important truth. "Winning" came in ways as different as the colors of horses. And winning with God was even better than winning a blue ribbon. Of this she was very sure.

"Nah, I'm not the best," Skye said with a winning smile. "God is. I'm just here to help."

A Letter to my Keystone Stables Fans

Dear Reader,

Are you crazy about horses like I am? Are you fortunate enough to have a horse now, or are you dreaming about the day when you will have one of your very own?

I've been crazy about horses ever since I can remember. When I was a child, I lived where I couldn't have a horse. Even if I had lived in the country, my folks didn't have the money to buy me one. So, as I grew up in a small coal town in central Pennsylvania, I dreamed about horses and collected horse pictures and horse models. I drew horse pictures and wrote horse stories, and I read every horse book I could get my hands on.

For Christmas when I was ten, I received a leather-fringed western jacket and a cowgirl hat. Weather permitting, I wore them when I walked to and from school. On the way, I imagined that I was riding a gleaming white steed into a world of mountain trails and forest paths.

Occasionally, during the summer, my mother took me to a riding academy where I rode a horse for one hour at a time. I always rubbed my hands (and hard!) on my mount before we left the ranch. For the rest of the day I tried not to wash my hands so I could smell the horse and remember the great time I had. Of course, I never could sit at the dinner table without Mother first sending me to the faucet to get rid of that "awful stench."

To get my own horse, I had to wait until I grew up, married, and bought a home in the country with enough land for a barn and a pasture. Moon Doggie, my very first horse, was a handsome brown and white pinto Welsh Mountain Pony. Many other equines came to live at our place where, in later years, my husband and I also opened our hearts to foster kids who needed a caring home. Most of the kids loved the horses as much as I did.

Although owning horses and rearing foster kids are now in my past, I fondly remember my favorite steed, who has long since passed from the scene. Rex, part Quarter Horse and part Tennessee Walker, was a 14 ½ hands-high bay. Rex was the kind of horse every kid dreams about. With a smooth walking gait, he gave me a thrilling ride every time I climbed into the saddle. Yet, he was so gentle, a young child could sit confidently on his back. Rex loved sugar cubes and nuzzled my pockets to find them. When cleaning his hooves, all I had to do was touch the target leg, and he lifted his hoof into my waiting hands. Rex was my special horse, and although he died at the ripe old age of twenty-five many years ago, I still miss him.

Rex

If you have a horse now or just dream about the day when you will, I beg you to do all you can to learn how to treat with tender love and respect one of God's most beautiful creatures. Horses make wonderful pets, but they require much more attention than a dog or a cat. For their loyal devotion to you, they only ask that you love them in return with the proper food, a clean barn, and the best of care.

Although Katie's story that you just read is fiction, the following pages contain horse facts that any horse lover will enjoy. It is my desire that these pages will help you to either care for your own horse better now or prepare you for that moment when you'll be able to throw your arms around that one special horse of your dreams that you can call your very own.

Happy riding!
Marsha Hubler

Are You Ready to Own Your First Horse?

The most exciting moment in any horse lover's life is to look into the eyes of a horse she can call her very own. No matter how old you are when you buy your first horse, it's hard to match the thrill of climbing onto his back and taking that first ride on a woodsy trail or dusty road that winds through open fields. A well-trained mount will give you a special friendship and years of pleasure as you learn to work with him and become a confident equestrian team.

But owning a horse involves much more than hopping on his back, racing him into a lather of sweat, and putting him back in his stall until you're ready to ride him again.

If you have your own horse now, you've already realized that caring for a horse takes a great amount of time and money. Besides feeding him twice a day, you must also groom him, clean his stall, "pick" his hooves, and have a farrier (a horseshoe maker and applier) and veterinarian make regular visits.

If you don't own a horse and you are begging your parents to buy one, please realize that you can't keep the horse in your garage and just feed him grass cuttings left over from a mowed lawn. It is a sad fact that too many neglected horses have ended up in rescue shelters after well-meaning families did not know how to properly care for their steeds.

If you feel that you are ready to have your own horse, please take time to answer the following questions. If you say yes to all of them, then you are well on your way to being the proud owner of your very own mount.

1. Do you have the money to purchase:
   - the horse? (A good grade horse can start at $800. Registered breeds can run into the thousands.)
   - a saddle, pad, and bridle, and a winter blanket or raincoat? ($300+ brand new)
   - a hard hat (helmet) and riding boots? ($150+)
   - essentials such as coat and hoof conditioner, bug repellent, electric clipper and grooming kit, saddle soap, First Aid kit, and vitamins? ($150+)

2. Does your family own at least a one-stall shed or barn and at least two acres of grass (enough pasture for one horse) to provide adequate grazing for your horse during warm months? If not, do you have the money to regularly purchase quality oats and alfalfa/timothy hay, and do you have the place to store the hay? Oh, and let's not forget the constant supply of sawdust or straw you need for stall bedding!

3. Are you ready to get up early enough every day to give your horse a bucket of fresh water, feed him a coffee can full of oats and one or two sections of clean dry hay (if you have no pasture), and "muck out" the manure from the barn?

4. Every evening, are you again ready to water and feed your horse, clean the barn, groom him, and pick his hooves?
5. Will you ride him at least twice a week, weather permitting?
6. If the answer to any of the above questions is no, then does your family have the money to purchase a horse and board him at a nearby stable? (Boarding fees can run as high as a car payment. Ask your parents how much that is.)

So, there you have the bare facts about owning and caring for a horse. If you don't have your own horse yet, perhaps you'll do as I did when I was young: I read all the books I could about horses. I analyzed all the facts about the money and care needed to make a horse happy. Sad as it made me feel, I finally realized that I would have to wait until I was much older to assume such a great responsibility. And now years later, I can look back and say, "For the horse's sake, I'm very glad I did wait."

I hope you've made the decision to give your horse the best possible TLC that you can. That might mean improving his care now or waiting until you're older to get a horse of your own. Whatever you and your parents decide, please remember that the result of your efforts should be a happy horse. If that's the case, you will be happy too.

Let's Go Horse Shopping!

If you are like I was when I was younger, I dreamed of owning the most beautiful horse in the world. My dream horse, with his long-flowing mane and wavy tail dragging on the ground, would arch his neck and prance with only a touch of my hand on his withers or a gentle rub of my boot heel on his barrel. My dream horse was often different colors. Sometimes he was silvery white; other times he was jet black. He was often a pinto blend of the deepest chocolate browns, blacks, and whites. No matter what color he was, he always took me on a perfect ride, responding to my slightest commands.

When I was old enough to be responsible to care for my own steed, I already knew that the horse of my dreams was just that, the horse of my dreams. To own a prancing pure white stallion or a high-stepping coal-black mare, I would have to buy a Lipizzaner, American Saddle Horse, or an Andalusian. But those kinds of horses were either not for sale to a beginner with a tiny barn or they cost so much, I couldn't afford one. I was amazed to discover that there are about 350 different breeds of horses, and I had to look for a horse that was just right for me, possibly even a good grade horse (that means not registered) that was a safe mount. Color really didn't matter as long as the horse was healthy and gave a safe, comfortable ride. (But I'm not sure what my friends might have said if I had a purple horse. That certainly would have been a "horse of a different color!") Then I had to decide if I wanted to ride western or English style. Well, living in central Pennsylvania farm country with oodles of trails and dirt roads, the choice for me was simple: western.

I'm sure if you don't have your own horse yet, you've dreamed and thought a lot about what your first horse will be. Perhaps you've already had a horse, but now you're thinking of buying another one. What kind should you get?

Let's look at some of the breeds that are the most popular for both western and English riders today. We'll briefly trace a few breeds' roots and characteristics while you decide if that kind of horse might be the one for you. Please keep in mind that this information speaks to generalities of the breeds. If given the proper care and training, most any breeds of horses make excellent mounts as well.

Some Popular Breeds (Based on Body Confirmation)

The Arabian

Sometimes called "The China Doll of the Horse Kingdom," the Arabian is known as the most beautiful of horse breeds because of its delicate features. Although research indicates Arabians are the world's oldest and purest breed, it is not known whether they originated in Arabia. However, many Bible scholars believe that the first horse that God created in the Garden of Eden must have embodied the strength and beauty that we see in the Arabian horse of today. It is also believed that all other breeds descended from this gorgeous breed that has stamina as well as courage and intelligence.

A purebred Arabian has a height of only 14 or 15 hands, a graceful arch in his neck, and a high carriage in his tail. It is easy to identify one of these horses by examining his head. If you see a small, delicate "dish" face with a broad forehead and tiny muzzle, two ears that point inward and large eyes that are often ringed in black, you are probably looking at an Arabian. The breed comes in all colors, (including dappled and some paint), but if you run your finger against the grain of any pureblood Arabian's coat, you will see an underlying bed of black skin. Perhaps that's why whites are often called "grays."

Generally, Arabians are labeled spirited and skittish, even though they might have been well trained. If you have your heart set on buying an Arabian, make sure you first have the experience to handle a horse that, although he might be loyal, will also want to run with the wind.

The Morgan

The Morgan Horse, like a Quarter Horse (see below), can explode into a gallop for a short distance. The Morgan, with its short legs, muscles, and fox ears, also looks very much like the Quarter Horse. How can we tell the two breeds apart?

A Morgan is chunkier than a Quarter Horse, especially in his stout neck. His long, wavy tail often flows to the ground. His trot is quick and short and with such great stamina, he can trot all day long.

So where are the Morgan's roots?

The horse breed was named after Justin Morgan, a frail music teacher who lived in Vermont at the turn of the eighteenth century. Instead of receiving cash for a debt owed, Mr. Morgan was given two colts. The smallest one, which he called Figure, was an undersized dark bay with a black mane and tail. Mr. Morgan sold the one colt, but he kept Figure, which he thought was a cross between a Thoroughbred and an Arabian. Over the years, he found the horse to be strong enough to pull logs and fast enough to beat Thoroughbreds in one afternoon and eager to do it all over again the same day!

When Mr. Morgan died, his short but powerful horse was called "Justin Morgan" in honor of his owner. After that, all of Justin Morgan's foals were called Morgans. The first volume of the Morgan Horse Register was published in 1894. Since then, hundreds of thousands of Morgans have been registered.

If you go Morgan hunting, you will find the breed in any combination of blacks, browns, and whites. Don't look for a tall horse because all Morgans are between 14 and 15 hands tall, just right for beginners. If you're fortunate enough to find a well-trained Morgan, he'll give you years of pleasure whether you ask him to gallop down a country trail, pull a wagon, or learn to jump obstacles.

The Mustang

If you want a taste of America's Wild West from days gone by, then you should treat yourself to the "Wild Horse of America," the Mustang.

This 14–15 hand, stout horse has its roots from Cortez and the Spanish conquistadors from the sixteenth century.

Although the Mustang's name comes from the Spanish word, *mesteno*, which means "a stray or wild grazer," he is most well known as the horse of the Native Americans. Numerous tribes all over the western plains captured horses that had escaped from their Spanish owners and ran wild. The Native Americans immediately claimed the Mustang as a gift from their gods and showed the world that the horse was, and is, easy to train once domesticated.

It didn't take long for the white settlers to discover the versatility of the Mustang. Because of his endurance, this little horse soon became a favorite for the Pony Express, the U.S. cavalry, cattle round-ups, and caravans.

Since the 1970s, the U.S. Bureau of Land Management has stepped in to save the Mustangs from extinction. As a result, herds of Mustangs still roam freely in U.S. western plains today. At different times of the year and in different parts of the country, the Adopt-a-Horse-or-Burro Program allows horse lovers to take a Mustang or burro home for a year and train it to be a reliable mount. After the year, the eligible family can receive a permanent ownership title from the government. As of October 2007, more than 218,000 wild horses and burros have been placed into private care since the adoption program began in 1973.

If you'd like a "different" kind of horse that sometimes has a scrubby look but performs with the fire of the Arab-barb blood, then go shopping for a Mustang. You'll find him in any black, brown, or white combination and with the determination and stamina to become your best equine friend.

The Quarter Horse

There's no horse lover anywhere in the world who hasn't heard of the American Quarter Horse. In fact, the Quarter Horse is probably the most popular breed in the United States today.

But what exactly is a Quarter Horse? Is he only a quarter of a horse in size, therefore, just a pony? No, this fantastic breed isn't a quarter of anything!

The Quarter Horse originated in American colonial times in Virginia when European settlers bred their stout English workhorses with the Native Americans' Mustangs. The result? A short-legged but muscular equine with a broad head and little "fox" ears, a horse that has great strength and speed.

It didn't take long for the colonists and Native Americans to discover that their new crossbreed was the fastest piece of horseflesh in the world for a quarter of a mile. Thus, the breed was christened the American Quarter Horse and began to flourish. Besides running quick races, it also pulled wagons, canal boats, and plows. When the American West opened up, cowpokes discovered that the Quarter Horse was perfect for herding cattle and to help rope steers. Although it remained a distinct breed for over three hundred years in the U.S., the Quarter Horse was only recognized with its own studbook in 1941.

If you are looking for a reliable mount that has a comfortable trot and smooth gallop, you might want to look at some *seasoned* Quarter Horses. (That means they have been trained properly and are at least five or six years old.) They come in any color or combination of colors. Their temperament is generally friendly, yet determined to get the job done that you ask them to do.

The Shetland Pony

Many beginning riders incorrectly believe that the smaller the horse, the easier it is to control him. You might be thinking, "I'm tiny, so I need a tiny horse!" But many beginners have found out the hard way that a Shetland Pony is sometimes no piece of cake.

Shetland Ponies originated as far back as the Bronze Age in the Shetland Isles, northeast of mainland Scotland.

Research has found that they are related to the ancient Scandinavian ponies. Shetland Ponies were first used for pulling carts, carrying peat and other items, and plowing farmland. Thousands of Shetlands also worked as "pit ponies," pulling coal carts in British mines in the mid–nineteenth century. The Shetland found its way at the same time to the United States when they were imported to also work in mines.

The American Shetland Pony Club was founded in 1888 as a registry to keep the pedigrees for all the Shetlands that were being imported from Europe at that time.

Shetlands are usually only 10.2 hands or shorter. They have a small head, sometimes with a dished face, big Bambi eyes, and small ears. The original breed has a short, muscular neck, stocky bodies, and short, strong legs. Shetlands can give you a bouncy ride because of their short broad backs and deep girths. These ponies have long thick manes and tails, and in winter climates their coats of any color can grow long and fuzzy.

If you decide you'd like to own a Shetland, spend a great deal of time looking for one that is mild mannered. Because of past years of hard labor, the breed now shows a dogged determination that often translates into stubbornness. So be careful, and don't fall for that sweet, fuzzy face without riding the pony several times before you buy him. You might get a wild, crazy ride from a "shortstuff" mount that you never bargained for!

The Tennessee Walking Horse

If you buy a Tennessee Walker, get ready for a thrilling ride as smooth as running water!

The Tennessee Walking Horse finds its roots in 1886 in Tennessee, when a Standardbred (a Morgan and Standardbred trotter cross) stallion named Black Allan refused to trot; instead, he chose to amble or "walk" fast. With effortless speed comparable to other horses' trots,

Black Allan's new gait (each hoof hitting the ground at a different time) amazed the horse world. Owners of Thoroughbreds and saddle horses were quick to breed their mares to this delightful new "rocking-horse" stud, and the Tennessee Walker was on its way to becoming one of the most popular breeds in the world. In just a few short years, the Walker became the favorite mount of not only circuit-riding preachers and plantation owners, but ladies riding sidesaddle as well.

Today the Walker, which comes in any black, brown, or white color or combination, is a versatile horse and is comfortable when ridden English or Western. He is usually 15 to 17 hands tall and has a long neck and sloping shoulders. His head is large but refined, and he has small ears. Because he has a short back, his running walk, for which he is known, comes naturally.

If you go shopping for a Tennesee Walker, you will find a horse that is usually mild mannered yet raring to go. Although most walkers are big and you might need a stepstool to climb on one, you will be amazed at how smooth his walk and rocking-horse canter is. In fact, you might have trouble making yourself get off!

Some Popular Breeds (Based on Body Color)

The Appaloosa

French cave paintings thousands of years old have "spotted" horses among its subjects, ancient China had labeled their spotted horses as "heavenly," and Persians have called their spotted steeds "sacred." Yet the spotted Appaloosa breed that we know today is believed to have originated in the northwestern Native Americans tribe called the Nez Perce in the seventeenth century.

When colonists expanded the United States territory westward, they found a unique people who lived near the Palouse River (which runs from north central Idaho to the Snake River in southeast Washington State). The Nez

Perce Indian tribe had bred a unique horse—red or blue roans with white spots on the rump. Fascinated, the colonists called the beautiful breed *palousey*, which means "the stream of the green meadows." Gradually, the name changed to *Appaloosa*.

The Nez Perce people lost most of their horses following the end of the Nez Perce War in 1877, and the breed started to decline for several decades. However, a small number of dedicated Appaloosa lovers kept the breed alive. Finally, a breed registry was formed in 1938. The Appaloosa was named the official state horse of Idaho in 1975.

If you decide to buy an Appaloosa, you'll own one of the most popular breeds in the United States today. It is best known as a stock horse used in a number of western riding events, but it's also seen in many other types of equestrian contests as well. So if you would like to ride English or Western, or want to show your horse or ride him on a mountain trail, an Appaloosa could be just the horse for you.

Appaloosas can be any solid base color, but the gorgeous blanket of spots that sometimes cover the entire horse identifies the special breed. Those spotted markings are not the same as pintos or the "dapple grays" and some other horse colors. For a horse to be registered as a pureblood Appaloosa, it also has to have striped hooves, white outer coat (sclera) encircling its brown or blue eyes, and mottled (spotted) skin around the eyes and lips. The Appaloosa is one of the few breeds to have skin mottling, and so this characteristic is a surefire way of identifying a true member of the breed.

In 1983, the Appaloosa Horse Club in America decided to limit the crossbreeding of Appaloosas to only three main confirmation breeds: the Arabian, the American Quarter Horse, and the Thoroughbred. Thus, the Appaloosa color breed also became a true confirmation breed as well.

If you want your neighbors to turn their heads your way when you ride past, then look for a well-trained Appaloosa. Most registered "Apps" are 15 hands or shorter but are full of muscle and loaded with spots. Sometimes, though, it takes several years for an Appaloosa's coat to mature to its full color. So if it's color you're looking for, shop for a seasoned App!

The Pinto

The American Pinto breed has its origins in the wild Mustang of the western plains. The seventeenth and eighteenth century Native Americans bred color into their "ponies," using them for warhorses and prizing those with the richest colors. When the "Westward Ho" pioneers captured wild Mustangs with flashy colors, they bred them to all different breeds of European stock horses. Thus, the Pinto has emerged as a color breed, which includes all different body shapes and sizes today.

The Pinto Horse Association of America was formed in 1956, although the bloodlines of many Pintos can be traced three or four generations before then. The association doesn't register Appaloosas, draft breeds, or horses with mule roots or characteristics. Today more than 100,000 Pintos are registered throughout the U.S., Canada, Europe, and Asia.

Pintos have a dark background with random patches of white and have two predominant color patterns:

1. Tobiano (Toe-bee-ah'-no) Pintos are white with large spots of brown or black color. Spots can cover much of the head, chest, flank, and rump, often including the tail. Legs are generally white, which makes the horse look like he's white with flowing spots of color. The white usually crosses the center of the back of the horse.

2. Overo (O-vair'-o) Pintos are colored horses with jagged white markings that originate on the animal's side or belly and spread toward the neck, tail, legs, and back. The deep, rich browns or blacks appear to frame the white. Thus, Overos often have dark backs and dark legs. Horses with bald or white faces are often Overos. Their splashy white markings on the rest of their body make round, lacy patterns.

Perhaps you've heard the term *paint* and wonder if that kind of horse is the same as a Pinto. Well, amazingly, the two are different breeds! A true Paint horse (registered by the American Paint Horse Association) must be bred from pureblood Paints, Quarter Horses, or Thoroughbreds. The difference in eligibility between the two registries has to do with the bloodlines of the horse, not its color or pattern.

So if you're shopping for a flashy mount and you don't care about a specific body type of horse, then set your sites on a Pinto or Paint. You might just find a well-trained registered or grade horse that has the crazy colors you've been dreaming about for a very long time!

The Palomino

No other color of horse will turn heads his way than the gorgeous golden Palomino. While the average person thinks the ideal color for a Palomino is like a shiny gold coin, the Palomino breed's registry allows all kinds of coat colors as long as the mane and tail are silvery white. A white blaze can be on the face but can't extend beyond the eyes. The Palomino can also have white stockings, but the white can't extend beyond the knees. Colors of Palominos can range from a deep, dark chocolate to an almost-white cremello. As far as body confirmation, four breeds are strongly represented in crossbreeding with the

Palomino today: the American Saddlebred, Tennessee Walker, Morgan, and Quarter Horse.

No one is sure where the Palomino came from, but it is believed that the horse came from Spain. An old legend says that Isabella, queen of Spain in the late fifteenth century, loved her golden horses so much she sent one stallion and five mares across the Atlantic to start thriving in the New World. Eventually those six horses lived in what is now Texas and New Mexico, where Native Americans captured the horses' offspring and incorporated them into their daily lives. From those six horses came all the Palominos in the United States, which proves how adaptable the breed is in different climates.

Today you can find Palominos all over the world and involved in all kinds of settings from jumping to ranching to rodeos. One of their most popular venues is pleasing crowds in parades, namely the Tournament of Roses Parade in Pasadena, California, every New Year's Day.

Perhaps you've dreamed of owning a horse that you could be proud of whether you are trail riding on a dirt road, showing in a western pleasure class, or strutting to the beat of a band in a parade. If that's the case, then the Palomino is the horse for you!

If you're shopping for the best in bloodlines, look for a horse that has a double registry! With papers that show the proper bloodlines, an Appaloosa Quarter Horse can be double registered. Perhaps you'd like a palomino Morgan or a pinto Tennessee Walker?

Who Can Ride a Horse?

As you have read this book about Skye, Morgan, and some of the other children with special needs, perhaps you could identify with one in particular. Do you have what society calls a handicap or disability? Do you use a wheelchair? Do you have any friends who are blind or have autism? Do you or your friends with special needs believe that none of you could ever ride a horse?

Although Keystone Stables is a fictitious place, there are real ranches and camps that connect horses with children just like Skye and Morgan, Sooze in book two, Tanya in book three, Jonathan in book four, Katie in book five, Joey in book six, and Wanda in book seven. That special kind of treatment and interaction has a long complicated name called Equine Facilitated Psychotherapy (EFP.)

EFP might include handling and grooming the horse, lunging, riding, or driving a horse-drawn cart. In an EFP program, a licensed mental health professional works together with a certified horse handler. Sometimes one EFP person can have the credentials for both. Whatever the case, the professionals are dedicated to helping both the child and the horse learn to work together as a team.

Children with autism benefit greatly because of therapeutic riding. Sometimes a child who has never been able to speak or "connect" with another person, even a parent, will bond with a horse in such a way that the child learns to relate to other people or starts to talk.

An author friend has told me of some of her family members who've had experience with horses and autistic children. They tell a story about a mute eight-year-old boy who was taking therapeutic treatment. One day as he was riding a well-trained mount that knew just what to do, the horse stopped for no reason and refused to budge. The leader said, "Walk on" and pulled on the halter, but the horse wouldn't move. The sidewalkers (people who help the child balance in the saddle) all did the same thing with the same result. Finally, the little boy who was still sitting on the horse shouted, "Walk on, Horsie!" The horse immediately obeyed.

So the good news for some horse-loving children who have serious health issues is that they might be able to work with horses. Many kids like Morgan, who has cerebral palsy, and blind Katie (book five) actually can learn to ride! That's because all over the world, people who love horses and children have started therapy riding academies to teach children with special needs how to ride and/or care for a horse. Highly trained horses and special equipment like high-backed saddles with Velcro strips on the fenders make it safe for kids with special needs to become skilled equestrians and thus learn to work with their own handicaps as they never have been able to do before!

A Word about Horse Whispering

If you are constantly reading about horses and know a lot about them, you probably have heard of horse whispering, something that many horse behaviorists do today to train horses. This training process is much different than what the majority of horsemen did several decades ago.

We've all read Wild West stories or seen movies in which the cowpoke "broke" a wild horse by climbing on his back and hanging on while the poor horse bucked until he was so exhausted he could hardly stand. What that type of training did was break the horse's spirit, and the horse learned to obey out of fear. Many "bronco busters" from the past also used whips, ropes, sharp spurs, and painful bits to make the horses respond, which they did only to avoid the pain the trainers caused.

Thankfully, the way many horses become reliable mounts has changed dramatically. Today many horses are trained, not broken. The trainer "communicates" with the horse using herd language. Thus, the horse bonds with his trainer quickly, looks to that person as his herd leader, and is ready to obey every command.

Thanks to Monty Roberts, the "man who listens to horses," and other professional horse whispering trainers like him, most raw or green horses (those that are just learning to respond to tack and a rider) are no longer broken.

Horses are now trained to accept the tack and rider in a short time with proven methods of horse whispering. Usually working in a round pen, the trainer begins by making large movements and noise as a predator would, encouraging the horse to run away. The trainer then gives the horse the choice to flee or bond. Through body language, the trainer asks the horse, "Will you choose me to be your herd leader and follow me?"

Often the horse responds with predictable herd behavior by twitching an ear toward his trainer then by lowering his head and licking to display an element of trust. The trainer mocks the horse's passive body language, turns his back on the horse, and, without eye contact, invites him to come closer. The bonding occurs when the horse chooses to be with the human and walks toward the trainer, thus accepting his leadership and protection.

Horse whispering has become one of the most acceptable, reliable, and humane ways to train horses. Today we have multitudes of rider-and-horse teams that have bonded in such a special way, both the rider and the horse enjoy each other's company. So when you're talking to your friends about horses, always remember to say the horses have been trained, not broken. The word *broken* is part of the horse's past and should remain there forever.

Bible Verses about Horses

Do you know there are about 150 verses in the Bible that include the word *horse*? It seems to me that if God mentioned horses so many times in the Bible, then he is very fond of one of his most beautiful creatures.

Some special verses about horses in the Bible make any horse lover want to shout. Look at this exciting passage from the book of Revelation that tells us about a wonderful time in the future:

"I saw heaven standing open and there before me was a white horse, whose rider is called Faithful and True. With justice he judges and makes war. His eyes are like blazing fire, and on his head are many crowns. He has a name written on him that no one knows but he himself. He is dressed in a robe dipped in blood, and his name is the Word of God. The armies of heaven were following him riding on white horses and dressed in fine linen, white and clean" (Revelation 19:11–14).

The rider who is faithful and true is the Lord Jesus Christ. The armies of heaven on white horses who follow Jesus are those who have accepted him as their Lord and Savior. I've accepted Christ, so I know that some day I'll get to ride a white horse in heaven. Do you think he will be a Lipizzaner, an Andalusian, or an Arabian? Maybe it will be a special new breed of white horses that God is preparing just for that special time.

Perhaps you never realized that there are horses in heaven. Perhaps you never thought about how you could go to heaven when you die. You can try to be as good as gold, but the Bible says that to go to heaven, you must ask Jesus to forgive your sins. Verses to think about: "For all have sinned and fall short of the glory of God" (Romans 3:23); "For God so loved the world that he gave his one and only son, that whoever believes in him shall not perish but have eternal life (John 3:16); "For everyone who calls on the name of the Lord will be saved" (Romans 10:13).

Do you want to be part of Jesus' cavalry in heaven some day? Have you ever asked Jesus to forgive your sins and make you ready for heaven? If you've never done so, please ask Jesus to save your soul today.

As I'm riding my prancing white steed with his long wavy mane and tail dragging to the ground, I'll be looking for you!

Glossary of Gaits

Gait–A gait is the manner of movement; the way a horse goes.

There are four natural or major gaits most horses use: walk, trot, canter, and gallop.

Walk–In the walk, the slowest gait, hooves strike the ground in a four-beat order: right hind hoof, right fore (or front) hoof, left hind hoof, left fore hoof.

Trot–In the trot, hooves strike the ground in diagonals in a one-two beat: right hind and left forefeet together, left hind and right forefeet together.

Canter–The canter is a three-beat gait containing an instant during which all four hooves are off the ground. The foreleg that lands last is called the *lead* leg and seems to point in the direction of the canter.

Gallop–The gallop is the fastest gait. If fast enough, it's a four-beat gait, with each hoof landing separately: right hind hoof, left hind hoof just before right fore hoof, left fore hoof.

Other gaits come naturally to certain breeds or are developed through careful breeding.

Running walk–This smooth gait comes naturally to the Tennessee walking horse. The horse glides between a walk and a trot.

Pace–A two-beat gait, similar to a trot. But instead of legs pairing in diagonals as in the trot, fore and hind legs on one side move together, giving a swaying action.

Slow gait–Four beats, but with swaying from side to side and a prancing effect. The slow gait is one of the gaits used by five-gaited saddle horses. Some call this pace the *stepping pace* or *amble*.

Amble–A slow, easy gait, much like the pace.

Rack–One of the five gaits of the five-gaited American saddle horse, it's a fancy, fast walk. This four-beat gait is faster than the trot and is very hard on the horse.

Jog–A jog is a slow trot, sometimes called a *dogtrot*.

Lope–A slow, easygoing canter, usually referring to a western gait on a horse ridden with loose reins.

Fox trot–An easy gait of short steps in which the horse basically walks in front and trots behind. It's a smooth gait, great for long-distance riding and characteristic of the Missouri fox trotter.

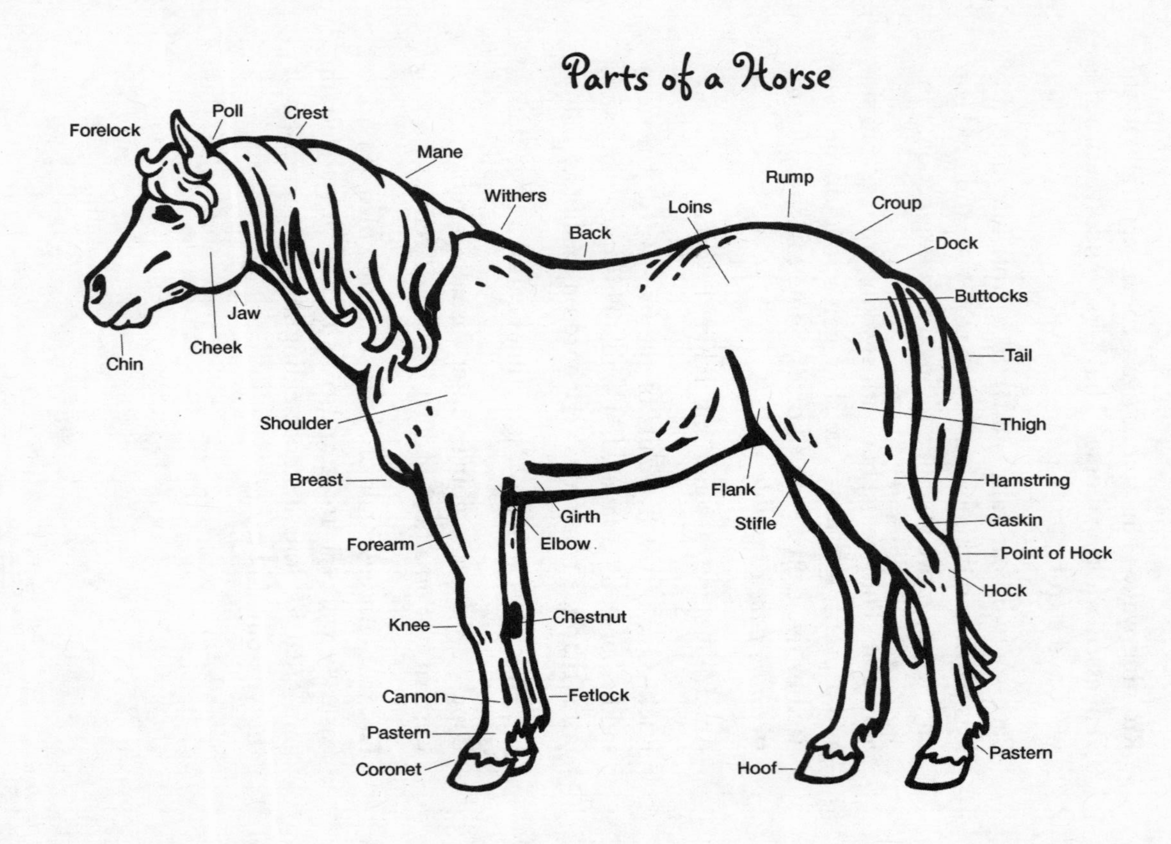
Parts of a Horse
Forelock
Poll
Crest
Mane
Withers
Back
Loins
Rump
Croup
Dock
Buttocks
Tail
Thigh
Hamstring
Gaskin
Point of Hock
Hock
Pastern
Hoof
Stifle
Flank
Girth
Elbow
Chestnut
Fetlock
Chin
Jaw
Cheek
Shoulder
Breast
Forearm
Knee
Cannon
Pastern
Coronet

The Western Saddle

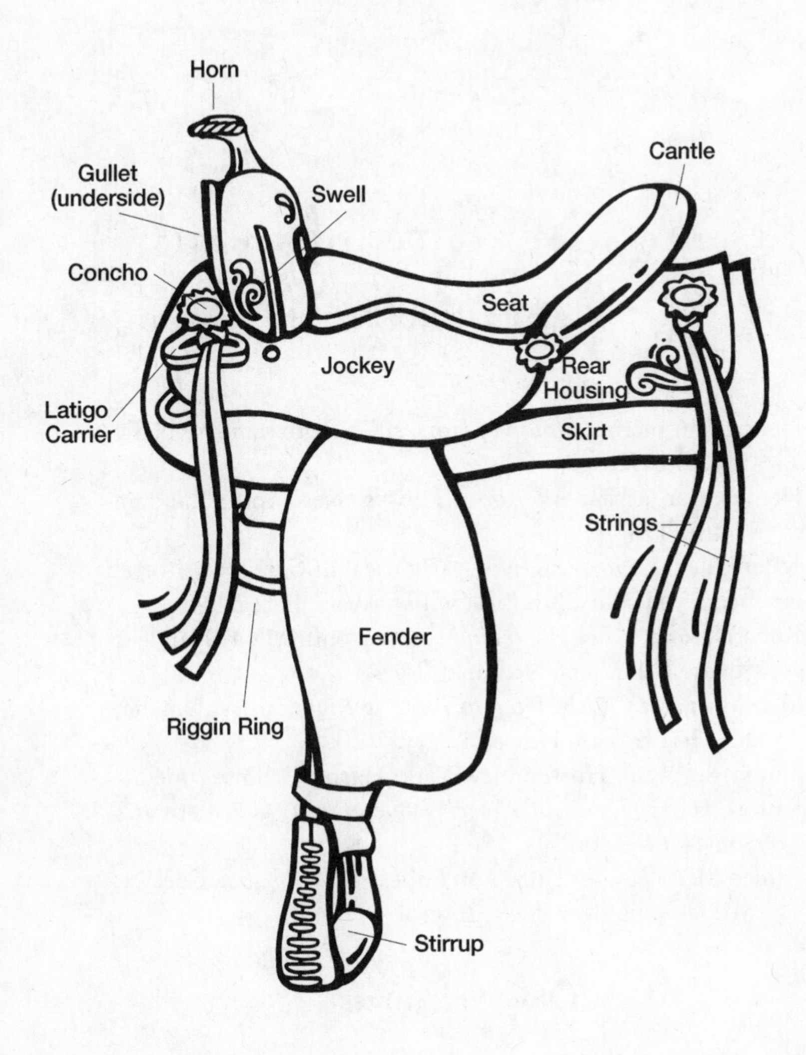

Resources for Horse Information Contained in this Book

Henry, Marguerite. *Album of Horses*. Chicago: Rand McNally & Co., 1952.

Henry, Marguerite. *All About Horses*. New York: Random House, 1967.

Jeffery, Laura. *Horses: How to Choose and Care for a Horse*. Berkley Heights, NJ: Enslow Publishers, Inc., 2004.

Roberts, Monty. *The Horses in My Life*. Pomfret, VT: Trafalgar Square Publishers, North, 2004.

Self, Margaret Cabell. *How to Buy the Right Horse*. Omaha, NE: The Farnam Horse Library, 1971.

Simon, Seymour. *Horses*. New York: HarperCollins, 2006.

Sutton, Felix. *Horses of America*. New York: G.P. Putnam's Sons, New York City, 1964.

Ulmer, Mike. *H is for Horse: An Equestrian Alphabet*. Chelsea, MI: Sleeping Bear Press, 2004.

Online resources

http://www.appaloosayouth.com/index.html
http://www.shetlandminiature.com/kids.asp
http://www.twhbea.com/youth/youthHome.aspx

Keystone Series

Written by Marsha Hubler

Check out the other books in the series!

Book 1: A Horse to Love
ISBN 978-0-310-71792-8

Book 2: On the Victory Trail
ISBN 978-0-310-71793-5

Book 3: Southern Belle's Special Gift
ISBN 978-0-310-71794-2

Book 4: Summer Camp Adventure
ISBN 978-0-310-71795-9

Book 5: Leading the Way
ISBN 978-0-310-71796-6

Book 6: Blue Ribbon Champ
ISBN 978-0-310-71797-3

Book 7: Whispering Hope
ISBN 978-0-310-71691-4
Coming May 2010

Book 8: The Long Ride Home
ISBN 978-0-310-71692-1
Coming May 2010

Available now at your local bookstore!

Sophie Series

Written by Nancy Rue

Meet Sophie LaCroix, a creative soul who's destined to become a great film director someday. But many times, her overactive imagination gets her in trouble!

Book 1: Sophie's World
IBSN: 978-0-310-70756-1

Book 2: Sophie's Secret
ISBN: 978-0-310-70757-8

Book 3: Sophie Under Pressure
ISBN: 978-0-310-71840-6

Book 4: Sophie Steps Up
ISBN: 978-0-310-71841-3

Book 5: Sophie's First Dance
ISBN: 978-0-310-70760-8

Book 6: Sophie's Stormy Summer
ISBN: 978-0-310-70761-5

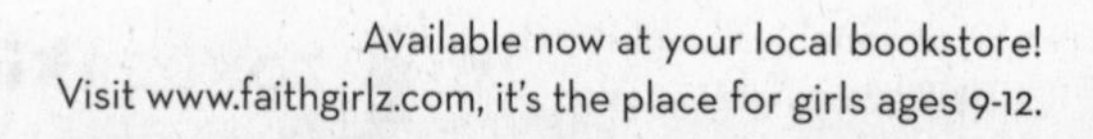

Sophie Series

Written by Nancy Rue

Book 7: Sophie's Friendship Fiasco
ISBN: 978-0-310-71842-0

Book 8: Sophie and the New Girl
ISBN: 978-0-310-71843-7

Book 9: Sophie Flakes Out
ISBN: 978-0-310-71024-0

Book 10: Sophie Loves Jimmy
ISBN: 978-0-310-71025-7

Book 11: Sophie's Drama
ISBN: 978-0-310-71844-4

Book 12: Sophie Gets Real
ISBN: 978-0-310-71845-1

Available now at your local bookstore!
Visit www.faithgirlz.com, it's the place for girls ages 9-12.

Boarding School Mysteries

Written by Kristi Holl

The Boarding School Mysteries series challenges twelve-year-old Jeri McKane, a sixth grader at the private Landmark School for Girls, to trust God's Word and direction as this amateur sleuth searches for clues in the midst of danger.

Fading Tracks
ISBN 978-0-310-71429-3

Smoke Screen
ISBN 978-0-310-71431-6

Secrets For Sale
ISBN 978-0-310-71430-9

Pick Your Poison
ISBN 978-0-310-71432-3

Available now at your local bookstore!
Visit www.faithgirlz.com, it's the place for girls ages 9-12.

ZONDERkidz.com